Ain't nobody's business if i do...

Ain't Nobody's Business If I Do

"I can't say enough about the writing itself in *Nobody's Business If I Do*. It is excellent throughout. The whole book is captivating. There is so much more I want to see and know about these people and this place. This is good, important work."

—Sara Combs, author of *Breakfast Served Anytime* and *The Light Fantastic*

"Your poem, *Where I Come From*, grabbed me by the ears and crammed my head into your tears, your dreams, your heartbreaks and your hopes. You pushed me down this path of your past… and any book for which this is the outline might well be great. Bring it on!'

—Dan Martin, former editor and publisher with Gannett; founding staffer for USA Today; former president and publisher of News-Press, Fort Myers

"These stories read like little movies. I can vividly see, hear and feel the characters. The author creates a richly evocative sense of place and time. Beautiful details of artifacts like the Wurlitzer jukebox, popular music and clothing put us in the moment. My favorite is Billie—I don't know anyone like her but feel I've met her in these pages. A unique and memorable character."

—Elaina Zuker, bestselling author

Dedicated to
My grandmother

Rebecca (Billie) Spriggs Brownie Gartin

RABBIT HOUSE PRESS
Versailles, KY 40383

For inquiries about author appearances and/or volume orders contact: rabbithousepress@gmail.com

ISBN: 979-8-9871928-7-0

Editors: Leatha Kendrick and Vickie Elkins
Cover Design: Miki Wright
Interior Design: Corbyn Keys & Brooke Lee

Ain't nobody's business if i do...

Janet Steele Holloway

Special Thanks to

The teachers, staff and writers at Lexington, KY's Carnegie Center for Literacy & Learning, the Senior Center's Life Writing Class, Leatha Kendrick, my editor and friend, Jean Welch, John Johnson, Pam Brinegar, Neil Chethik, Don & Ellen Branscome

CONTENTS

*These stories made an earlier appearance in my first book, *A Willful Child*, but have been modified for this selection.

PROLOGUE

After two memoirs, in which I try my best to tell the truth as I know it, people asked, "What's next?" I didn't have an answer, until a couple of years after publishing *Leaving: Sometimes You Have to Leave*. I realized that the old folks I grew up with were still in my head. They were wreaking havoc and having fun teasing me about stories I knew little about. Finally, I sat down to write what I could, not at all certain I was near the truth. I decided to describe this book as autobiographical fiction, where the characters are real but in situations that are imagined. It's the best I could do with them.

In these stories, I am often a narrator—a young girl who has seen way too much, too early in her life, tossed between the conflict and instability of her parents' relationship and the steady love of her grandmother—a liberated woman long before the concept was popular. She—my Granny Bill—was the strength I needed as a child. Four stories – *Nobody's Business If I Do, Bess' Story, The Rose Room and Straighten Up and Fly Right* – are as close to the truth as I can get. Granny always took my side, taught me I could achieve whatever I wanted in life, if I were willing to work hard and apply myself. I am the person I am today as a result of her steadfast love and support, and her story still inspires me.

These stories are an attempt to capture her impact on others in the large, extended Appalachian family.

Where I Come From

I come from Hatfield land where legend is a close neighbor,
  where *old Devil Anse Hatfield will git you* if you break the rules
  or disobey your elders,
  where someone you know is a cousin, nephew, stepbrother, half-
  sister—part of the original clan;
  where a taller than life-sized statue, cut in creamy Carrera
  marble, stands high on the closest hill, amid pokeberry and
  poison ivy, surveying all that was once his land,
  where occasional tourists climb a weeded path to show respect
  or swap stories about the feud.

I come from a haunted place.

I come from creeks and valleys and hollers, narrow as a ribbon,
  some reached through noisy streams and muddy climbs,
  shaded by the color of poplars and sugar maples,
  infused with the scent of rotting earth.

I come from deep pools of creek water where we were baptized
  in the fall and swam in summer in spite of warnings about water
  moccasins.

I come from hillbillies,
  barely educated families who ate the food they grew,
  passed down used clothes and shoes, well past dreaming
  of a future.

I come from men who drilled seams of black coal,
    and women who served beers to drooling customers with
    broken backs and nameless sins.

I come from one-room churches,
    where women were saved at the front altar and
    teens, in the back row, leafed through hymnals and Bibles
    whispering *under the bed* to song titles like *Softly and Tenderly*
    or words like Jesus Saves *under the bed*.

I come from furnished apartments and coal camp houses,
    where front porches and windows, imprinted with carbon soot,
    required repeated cleaning each day,
    where we played hide and seek in alleyways
    and threw eggs and firecrackers on Halloween.

I come from a mother who knew nothing about her birth family,
    who suffered from what doctors called "nerves,"
    and who treated her with valium and lithium,
    while she treated herself to alcohol and sad escapes from our
    family life.

I come from a father who labored underground and who always
    took her back.

I come from a time where trouble came from within families
    and kids were parceled out for protection,
    where alcohol drained life from strong men and fragile women.

I come from hot summers working on my grandmother's farm in
    the Knobs of Virginia,
    a home without running water or indoor niceties,
    time spent working tobacco fields, hiding in apple orchards,
    learning to dream;
    a place where I felt needed and free.

I come from teachers who told me I was smart,
    that I needed to read and study and stay in school.

I come from schools here and there, each year a different one,
    a different state,
    learning about the wider world, and about loneliness
    and being on my own from an early age,
    grasping at friendships, bundling into others' families for warmth.

I come from a moonshining grandmother who carried a gun,
    who loaned money and gave respite,
    who fed and clothed those who needed it,
    bought votes at election time to ensure her point of view,
    who knew most people's secrets,
    and used her power to protect and get even.

I come from the unrestrained yet tough love of this grandmother,
    who taught me to be strong,
    to stand up for what I believed,
    to care for others.

I may not be of her seed, but I am of her heart.

CHAPTER 1

Billie's Memorial Reception

Helen held open the torn screen door, waving her rough chapped hand to the couple who, except for family, were last to leave the after-funeral reception.

"You all come back now; you hear?"

She let the patched screen door slam shut and shuffled to the kitchen and her faded, plaid chair opposite the Formica table. She picked up a cigarette from the small table beside her. "Whew! That was an awful lot of people come to say goodbye to Billie!"

Preston, Helen's grown son, bent down to light her cigarette and hand her an ash tray more than half filled with butts and ash.

"Empty that crap out of there before giving it to me," Helen said sharply, waving him away. "Don't you have no manners?" she groaned.

He did as she asked, ran some cold water over the ash tray, dried it with a greasy dish towel and handed it back to her.

"You done real good today, Mama," Preston lisped. "I know you didn't want to have everybody over here, but you done real good."

"Billie might have appreciated it had she been here," Roosevelt, Helen's brother, said. He and a few other family members sat around the oval turquoise kitchen table. Everyone murmured their agreement.

There were six or seven immediate family members sitting around the house, some coming into the kitchen, from time to time to sample another dish provided by Helen's neighbors or to or add ice to their paper cups of Four Roses. Cousin Donald sat with two geriatric female cousins, talking in the shadowed living room. When it was quiet in the kitchen, you could hear them talking about

Billie's early life, during the Depression and Prohibition days. Their conversation and disapproving clucks wafted through the dining room and into the space of the kitchen drinkers.

"If you all want to drink," Helen called out, "I can open the bar. We got plenty of drink out there."

"Naw. It's too early yet," grinned Roosevelt, finishing off whatever was in his cup and whispering loudly to everyone in the room, "Maybe in a half hour or so," his smile showing evidence of missing teeth and a rough life. He moved his chair closer to the table.

Helen searched around in her cotton dress pocket to produce a hefty set of keys. "Preston, take these keys and go over to the bar and get us a couple bottles of whisky and a six pack. Bring back some soda pop too. People here are getting thirsty." She eyed the nearly empty bottle next to the sink.

Nearly seventy with a wind-whipped complexion and curvy, sagging body, Helen had wild gray hair that no bobby pin could keep out of her eyes or behind her ears. She was Billie's younger sister. Like Billie, she owned what might be called a neighborhood bar just off the highway. That is, if the unincorporated village of Switzer, West Virginia, could be called a neighborhood with its seven hundred or so residents along Route 119, between the coal camps of Micco and Monaville.

Helen's bar was a slumping 600 square foot building, just a few steps from her front porch, and it could be identified a quarter mile away by a 3-foot-high purple neon H sign, nearly as wide as the building itself, secured on top of the roof. It was called Helen's Purple H Bar and the extended family often gossiped, when Helen wasn't around, that it was quite a few steps down from Billie's Pioneer Inn and Beer Garden up the road in Sarah Ann.

After Preston left for the drinks, a neighbor church member walked up on the porch, holding a Corning ware casserole dish. "Come on in," Helen called out.

Seeing what was going on in the kitchen, the plainly dressed woman protested, "No, no. Just something for the family." She opened the door and thrust the dish into Maggie's hands, practically running off the porch and barely avoiding a crash with Preston who had his arms full of liquor and beer. He yelled "Party in the kitchen; come on back."

"No, no," the neighbor squealed and walked faster.

Maggie held the door for Preston, then put the dish alongside several others on the laminated counter. Maggie was wearing a long-sleeved black dress with a white collar, thinking she was conforming to tradition by wearing black and she was sweating heavily. She wasn't family but she'd been around Billie for more than 40 years—working for her at the beer garden, cleaning the motel rooms, helping Billie when she suffered with her radium treatments. She had worked in a sanitarium in earlier years after Billie sold the beer garden. Everyone called Maggie cousin.

From the living room, one of the cousins called out an invite: "We're here talking about Billie. Ya'll come in here." She and the other cousin remained in the front room, serious and pious, separating themselves from what was developing in the kitchen.

"Well," shouted Helen, "So are we!" With no response, she added "Stay in there if you want; I don't care."

With effort, Helen pushed herself up and went to the refrigerator, removing two metal ice trays from the freezer. With an ash-laden cigarette between her lips, she put the trays in the sink, pulled the lever to release ice from the tray, and poured herself a hefty shot of Four Roses with one ice cube and a touch of Coke. She leaned on the back of Roosevelt's chair as she made her way back to her seat, leaving the chilled tray in the sink. "Ya'll help yourselves," she told them as she dropped her cigarette in the now half-full ashtray.

With the exception of the ice clunking into paper cups, it was quiet as people moved to the sink, then to sit around the kitchen table. The drink seemed to inject a pensiveness into the setting. Dusk was setting in, leaving slight shadows on the merry kitchen wallpaper. None of the lights were on. They listened to cousin Cora going on about one of Billie's escapades during Prohibition, along with cousin Effie's disapproving clucks.

It was several minutes before Roosevelt spoke. "I wouldn't know where to begin to tell stories about my sister. She was a good woman; she helped me and my family when we needed it." He rested his grizzled chin on his folded hands.

Maggie started to laugh—a deep, coarse, cigarette laugh, which made her cough in between her good humor—and pointed to Roosevelt. "Yes, and, before she died, Billie also made you marry Josey, didn't she?"

"Well," drawled Roosevelt, "She surely did. Billie didn't believe God could accept common law, no matter how many years you'd been together." He paused, as if lost in the past, took a drink and wiped his mouth with a Pabst Blue Ribbon napkin. "Josey and I'd had 40—45 years and six kids. Never saw a reason to sign papers. Still, it was the last thing she asked of me, and I felt I had to do it."

"You sure did," Helen interrupted. "What I heard was that Billie called the preacher that very day and told him to come over. You didn't have no choice, big brother."

Maggie put her head down on the table, still laughing. "Damn! That woman could get more done in a day than anyone else in a lifetime. And secrets? Lord 'a mercy, she had a way of finding out the true situation behind every person's story, didn't she?"

Helen stared at the bald spot on Maggie's head, visible in spite of her teased, dyed black hair. She started to say something when the screen door opened and Pauline, her younger half-sister came in, stopped to look around and put her hands on her hips.

"Hell's bells! Ya'll started the party without me! Get me a drink, Helen."

"Get your own damned drink, Pauline. Where you been? You stop off to see that man of yours?"

Pauline ignored the insult and pointed to Preston and then to the sink. He got up and poured her a straight whiskey. No ice.

"Thank you, darlin'," she said. "What ya'll talking about?"

Pauline was one of the prettier sisters, tall and thin, bleached blond hair kept in place with weekly appointments, and an overbite that gave her a devilish smile. No one could ignore Pauline when she was in the room.

"We're still talking about your sister, Billie," said Maggie, offering her seat to Pauline and moving toward the sink for a refill.

"God love her," Pauline sighed. "She was a wild one and bossy as hell. But she was always right, wasn't she? She got me in more trouble that I could find myself. And that's a lot." Downing her drink and offering the empty glass to Preston with a nod, she continued, "Don't ya'll remember all those times she'd get in her car and follow poor Bess to see where she was going?"

Maggie cackled, "Lord, yes! She loved to catch people up to no good."

"She used to scare the be-Jesus out of me when I was a kid," nephew Donald said, coming from the living room into the kitchen to give Pauline a hug. "She'd hide and put a sheet over her and jump out to scare us kids at night." Smiles spread across sad faces.

Helen looked down at the floor.

Pauline continued, "She used to get me to watch the beer garden while she'd get in her car to follow poor Bess, just to see where she was going." She went on, her voice getting higher as she spoke. "She was sure her daughter was fooling around, and, by god, she was going to stop her before it got back to Mel."

Helen shook her head; she didn't want to hear stories about Billie's daughter. "Pauline, stop telling lies now. You know Bess wasn't fooling around."

Maggie was feeling sassy by this time, her drinking starting to show itself as she struggled, half coughing to say, "Stop telling lies now, Pauline. Bess wasn't doing anything."

"Huh! How long you been blind, Maggie? Bess was always a big flirt. Preston, why are you so slow? Give me another of what you gave me before." She stood up and gave Preston a nod.

"Yes, ma'am, coming right up!"

Helen changed the subject. "Bess and her kids left after the funeral to drive back to Huntington, or she'd be here. She was pretty tore up."

"Didn't she look pretty though?" Pauline asked.

They all murmured in agreement.

Bess, now in her early 50's, was pretty. Beautiful, even. She'd had many suitors when she was in her twenties, even though she was married. Family photos showed the startling beauty she possessed— clear ivory skin, heavy dark auburn hair rolled up in hair rats and victory curls, a fashion of the early 40's, shiny green eyes. Her style was even more dramatic and promising once she applied ruby black lipstick to her full lips and mascara to her long lashes. Even though she had a husband and two children, men were drawn to her, encouraged by her looks, her laughter and the fact that she enjoyed the flirtation and flattery.

Helen, now trying to steer the conversation from Bess altogether, asked, "Whatever happened to that old man who lived across from Billie's place? Do we need to tell him about Billie's death?"

"Oh, you mean old Dogman who stayed in that shack on Hatfield land?" Maggie asked. "I haven't heard a thing about him for years."

"Who're we talking about?" Donald asked.

"We all called him Dogman. He was the old man who lived across from Billie's place of business. Never did know his name. He had a huge crush on Bess!" Pauline offered as she reached for the ice tray.

"Now stop it Pauline," Maggie raised her voice. "They weren't nothing wrong with that old man. He was just a loner, no place to live, no family. He never bothered nobody."

"I never said he did," Pauline sang out, lifting her shoulders and rolling her blue eyes.

"Fact is," Maggie continued, "Billie used to send him groceries or leftovers of something we'd cooked. She never worried about him and Bess."

"I didn't say she did," Pauline repeated and shrugged.

Roosevelt spoke up, "I remember him. He was a hermit and Billie let him live in that shack across the creek that she bought from the Hatfields. He used to send presents to Bess on Christmas or something, I believe. I was there one time and there was this flimsy dime store yellow nightgown on the bar that he'd sent her."

"Whoo hoo!" shouted Pauline.

"Aw, it was nothing." Maggie inserted. "Billie always laughed about it. Bess just liked the fact that it made Mel jealous. She didn't want anything to do with Dogman."

"As I recall," Helen said, "Bess and her family were living upstairs over the bar back in the 50's. The mines had closed down so Mel didn't have no work. I think Bess helped Billie out in the bar at the time."

"She sure did," Maggie said. "Mel didn't like it though. He'd always say, 'No wife of mine is going to have to work!'"

Pauline stood up and stretched. Helen handed her empty glass and the nearly full ashtray to Preston, the settled back into her chair, eyes closed. Maggie put her head down on the table, while Roosevelt raised himself from the chair and ambled toward the door with his unlit cigarette, saying he needed some air. Donald followed him onto the porch.

The room grew quiet; each of them thinking of ways Billie had touched their lives, their histories fused beyond truth with so many others.

CHAPTER TWO

Dogman

Dogman was not the dog/man/animal who haunts the imaginations of those in the northern peninsula of Michigan or the Cajun backwaters. He was simply an old hermit, poor as dirt, who inhabited the run-down, one room shack at the foot of the mountain, a few hundred feet from the Hatfield home place and, ultimately, my grandmother Billie's Pioneer Inn & Beer Garden. We kids were always told not to bother him and to never go into his shanty. We were also warned not to make fun of him: he was old, shabby and dirty with a long beard and we had to respect him as an elder. Or else.

He kept to himself, barely uttering a word to infrequent hunters who passed by, sharing his life with two large dogs of uncertain pedigree. He seldom left his home and could be seen, from time to time, on his makeshift porch taking in the sun, his dogs sleeping nearby. The shack had neither a shower nor toilet, so he had to walk into the woods when pressed, and he collected water from the relatively clean creek for drinking and washing up. It would be a great exaggeration to say he was clean. As a child, I was very curious about him but was told he's fine, just don't let him get too close to you.

The howling of his dogs resounded through the hollows at night, carried along by a whisper of wind, and giving a shiver to anyone unfamiliar with the area. The dogs did what dogs do: chase down the squirrel, opossum and fox, drag them back for Dogman's dinners, knowing that leftovers would be going to the soldiers of the hunt.

His memories traced back to when the leader of the Hatfields lived on the land. Anderson (Anse) Hatfield was a physically powerful man, six feet tall, with a full head of hair and a profuse beard and his sons favored him. Dogman knew the Hatfields well enough to keep to himself, although he'd often bring them rabbits or squirrels he'd shot while roaming the woods. They'd offer him a pint or jar of moonshine in return.

The Hatfield's log cabin was about 500 feet away from Dogman's place, down in the bottom land, by the creek, and a crowd of Anse's rough looking boys were stuffed into the small cabin, along with Levicy, Anderson's wife, and his two girls. When Dogman was younger, he had worked in the Hatfield's timber business, helping to cut trees and roll them down the mountain, to be taken to town for shipping by train. An unnamed mishap left him unable to continue.

The Hatfields kept an eye on him and let him live in the shanty. He had no place else to go so he stayed on. To our knowledge, he had no relatives or friends, and we had no idea where he came from.

Through the years, Dogman had listened to stories of the bloodshed between the Hatfields and the McCoys down in Kentucky and on the boarder of West Virginia, and he showed up when some of the boys were buried nearby. "I felt bad for them," he was said to have told a bystander at one funeral. "They was good people to me."

After the patriarch of the Hatfield family died in 1921, Dogman told Billie he had offered to help carry the casket the half mile down the road and up the hill to the cemetery. There were still enough boys around to do the job, so they thanked him but said no. When he related that story to Billie, he also told her he was shocked at all the people attending the funeral. It appears that a train came all the way to Hatfield Creek, loaded with people from Logan County and thereabouts who wanted to see Anse Hatfield buried. Newspapers heralded the crowd with front-page pictures, the grieving family in the forefront.

Billie wasn't there for the funeral but heard many stories from Hatfield friends and relatives who lived nearby and with whom Billie did business.

Soon after Hatfield's passing, some of the fighting continued but the boys wandered away from the home place and the fighting was piecemeal. It was said there was a still built under their homeplace and, somehow, it caught fire and blew up the house, leaving the bottom land to fill with weeds, frogs and thorns. There remained a number of relatives in the area, mostly cousins and uncles, brothers-in-law, but outside attraction lessened easily. The legend never died though, and Dogman was as close to it as anyone. Thanks to Billie and Arthur, her husband, Dogman remained in the shanty for many more years after Anse's death.

Granny Bill once told me that Dogman had helped my mother when she was in a car wreck a quarter mile from Granny's business. Dogman was in the woods and saw the car spin out of control and come to a stop in a ditch, radio blaring. He came out of the hills to see if folks in the car were all right and saw my mother there with an unknown man behind the wheel, drunk as could be. My mother was shaken but unhurt. Dogman took her to his shanty and left her by the fire while he went to find Billie. Granny went with him to get my mother, wanting to ensure that my dad, Mel, wouldn't know what had happened. According to her, everything worked out just fine, even though she gave my mother "what for" the next day.

Around the time of Anse's passing and the spread of the Depression, Billie had moved from Virginia with her husband Arthur Wesley Brownie, a railroad clerk and moonshiner. They settled in Hatfield Creek as it was then called. Billie had had a tough life, watching out for herself, her two brothers and four sisters and a tobacco farm during one of the harshest times in America. She was smart and cunning, and she and Arthur had good success in distributing the moonshine her siblings and her husband's family made, traveling to Chicago and Cleveland and Detroit to serve customers of the speakeasies up north.

Billie saw the Hatfield land as an opportunity to bring more people to the area and, for years, she tried to get Logan County officials to commercialize the area and graveyard as a tourist spot.

She recognized the importance of Hatfield history and the fact that many family members still lived in the area. The tourist spot was never developed until after her death.

Using money earned from the *shine* business, she negotiated a deal with a trustee of the Hatfields for the land at the head of what became known as Sarah Ann, right along the road, at $20 per acre. (See handwritten deed.) She planned to use a one-story concrete block building, left by the Hatfield's, as a supermarket and beer garden with cinder-block cabins alongside the building. Recognizing the opportunity, she decided to provide housing and food for the Works Project Administration (WPA) men working on the roads, cutting timber and mining coal in the area. The Hatfields had used the concrete building as a lock-up, often as a way to maintain control over the Hatfield boys when they were drunk and looking for trouble. Billie knew if she added a second floor to the building, there'd be living space for her and any family needing it. Given the darkness of the valley, she decided to create a large living room surrounded by glass on three sides. As it turned out, that room was lit by the neon sign that spelled out Pioneer Inn and Beer Garden. The room became magical for me as a child, where I poured through the Reader's Digest collection amid the changing red, blue and green colors of the sign. The addition would include a small kitchen and bathroom with five bedrooms opening off the long hall from the living room to the back stairs leading to the bar.

As they worked out the deal for the land, the trustee told Billie about Dogman and how he'd been close to the Hatfields. "I don't have any problem with him staying where he is," Billie told him, "As long as he don't make no trouble." Keeping her plans to herself and protecting the price they'd agreed upon, she told the trustee, "Right now, I don't have any plans to do anything with that bottom land."

In time, Billie set up a more-or-less legitimate business on the Hatfield land: a grocery and beer garden, with *shine* available to special customers in the back room, plus living space upstairs. Billie was always good at seeing opportunity.

Times were looking better: the feud had abated, timber and coal were needed throughout the country, and roads and other infrastructure were putting West Virginia on the map.

Eventually we lost track of Dogman. Where he went, we never knew, but he occasionally appeared in my dreams.

Devil Anse Hatfield, probably ca. 1910

Devil Anse's funeral, 1921

Dedication of statue marking Devil Anse's grave, ca. 1925

These three photographs show that in later life Devil Anse came to identify with the wealthier, urban segment of Logan County society. His new image is exemplified in the gentlemanly portrait, the frame house typical of town dwellers, and the Italian marble statue which he and his family thought appropriate in an otherwise unadorned and remote cemetery. (*Courtesy West Virginia Department of Culture and History, Charleston*)

CHAPTER THREE

Ain't Nobody's Business

Long before I was born, my grandmother, Billie, stood by the car, looking out over the Shenandoah valley, breathing in the slight breeze coming in from the soft mountains in the distance. She was looking forward to seeing her sister Kate and to check on the farm. Her sister had done a fine job of managing the old family place Billie had inherited years ago. Their visits were as much pleasure as business.

As Billie paid the sweaty gas station attendant, she caught a snatch of conversation between two women apparently talking of a baby for sale just down the road. That's absurd. Must be a dog, she thought, counting her change. Her car gleamed in the sun. Nearly new and paid for, it was a source of pride. All in all, Billie was in a fine mood. It's good to be back here, she murmured to herself. She smiled, remembering her years on the farm when she and her brothers and sisters worked the tobacco fields with their father. The hard work she'd learned to do in those days had become a lifelong habit. Work and pleasure went together for Billie.

The two women were now standing by the gas pumps, intense in their conversation. They were definitely talking about a baby for sale. "It cost $2.25 to fill up this car AND there's a baby for sale? This world's gone crazy," Billie muttered. She stood in the heat for a moment to hear more of what the women were saying. Soon enough she lost patience and interrupted them to ask if it was true.

A young, barefoot blonde plumped her short, wavy hair. A plastic hair comb caught the afternoon sun, blocking Billie's vision for a moment. In the glare, the blonde appeared ghostlike.

"Why, yes ma'am. It certainly is. The woman who has the baby lives just down there," pointing to a narrow road off the wider one they were on.

"What in the world? A baby for sale? Is she colored?"

"No ma'am," the blonde answered quickly.

The second woman, much older, gray hair in a braid, adjusted the cardboard box of vegetables on her hip, and spoke up, "I just heard someone say that a friend of this woman here had the baby out of wedlock and asked her friend here—I think her name is Meadows —to take her."

The woman wore a tee shirt and dirty overalls. No doubt she'd been working in the fields somewhere nearby. Hard work in this heat.

"What a shame," Billie said. Shaking her head, she turned away from the women with a nod of thanks. Settled into the car, she found a jazz station on the car radio and lit a cigarette, drawing deeply. It's a shame all around, but mostly for the baby. Either that woman who had her is crazy or desperate. What would make a woman sell her own baby? She was thoughtful for several minutes.

The smoke and the jazz music raced through her, adjusting a weight Billie didn't know she was carrying. The music soothed her. She'd gotten to like jazz in big cities like Chicago and sometimes on WXYZ, and she'd heard Bessie Smith singing in a speakeasy club one time. Bessie was now singing softly, so Billie turned up the volume and hummed along.

If I should take a notion, to jump right in the ocean,
'Taint nobody's business if I do.

The music and cigarette smoke led her down her own path of memory and her own suffering over the past couple of years. She had lost her three-month-old baby from pneumonia; then her husband disappeared. No one, least of all Billie, knew where Arthur had gone, or if he was still alive. The two of them had been in Chicago, making a delivery of *shine*, when he went out for razor blades one night and never came back. People said his disappearance had something to do with his moonshine business. Maybe a late delivery or bad-tasting juice. She had always accompanied Arthur when he made deliveries, loving the new experiences, the speak-easies, the dance halls.

In the late 1920's, moonshining had been a dependable source of income for Billie's folks for many years in Virginia and West Virginia. This tragedy of Arthur's disappearance left questions about the husband's real reasons for leaving, but the truth was never known. Not having any facts to go on, everyone accepted that he had run amok with the monied men in moonshining.

In spite of her personal losses, my grandmother was strong. At fourteen, she'd become responsible for raising her six younger siblings after her mother died, and still had to provide financial support for some. Plus, she not only had to take over her husband's business after he left her in Chicago, she had to carry on with the requirements of the tobacco farm left her when her father passed. She was the one the family depended on, the matriarch with six siblings, all of them acknowledging Billie held the purse strings and was in charge of most things. Managing everything kept her busy and kept the sadness at bay.

Yet sometimes the weight of these years and the sadness took her breath away. She'd have to stand very still or hold onto something when it came over her, like now. Sometimes she'd shudder, like she was back there for a moment and forgot where she was. These thoughts ran through her mind, driving her, unawares, deeper into this recent tragedy. The music changed from jazz to swing and Billie turned down the radio volume.

If the road's down this-away, she thought, as she turned the car onto a one lane dirt road, I think I'll go check this out. I want to see what's going on here.

At the same time, about 40 miles away, near downtown Abingdon, an attractive young woman named Hattie was preparing dinner for her tired husband and three children. Roger had had a long day's work: handling loan applications all day long as bank president, then coming home to mow one of the fields where they would grow corn.

Hattie had been away from home for several weeks, taking care of an ailing relative, she told everyone, and she was happy to be back. Neighbors and friends had come by earlier in the day to extend their sympathies for the family illness. They told Hattie they'd been praying for her. Hattie herself had no time for regret or guilty feelings. She had to get this meal of fried chicken and mashed potatoes on the table. It was summer and she had a whole month with her children before starting to teach again. Hattie was happy to be home with her family. She had missed them.

A few days later, Billie returned to Hatfield Creek, WV, where Arthur's business and their home were located. She had a pocketbook full of *shine* money and a baby on her shoulder.

Her sisters were sure she had lost her mind. "She's still grieving the loss of her boy," they whispered. "And then her husband leaving her like that...."

Everyone wanted to know. Where did this child come from? Who did she belong to? How did this come about? So much mystery in Billie's life.

Billie tolerated no gossip or even questions about the month-old child, giving everyone the same answer: "She's my baby, that's who she is. It's nobody else's business!"

She sent her younger sister Helen to find a crib and bedding, asked her child-prolific sister-in-law for some clothes and diapers, and had her brother, Roosevelt, move the furniture around in the large bedroom she had shared with Arthur to make room for the crib. She wanted everyone to meet her new baby and took her from one sister's house to another and to the neighbors and more. And, still, she was direct, even rude sometimes, if they asked who the baby was or where she came from.

Naming the girl became a snarky business, four jealous sisters throwing out ugly suggestions like Stinky and Shit Face and Orphan and even Jemima. Billie took her time to settle on a name because she wanted to get to know the child first. She ignored the sarcasm, or at least acted like it, paying no attention to their rattle.

After two or three days, Billie named her Bess. She had had an instinct about the name.

Still, everyone wanted to know how this child came about. Her brothers knew to stay away from the subject, turning aside or leaving the room when it came up. They were also known to raise an eyebrow or two when the women were talking. One even told his wife he wouldn't put it past Billie to trade *shine* for the infant.

Billie remained stoic regarding Bess, put up with no gossip, no questions, and as matriarch and major supporter of the family, her word was law; she gave everyone the same reply: "She's my baby."

Days went by with Billie going around with Bess in her sling. She'd had a neighbor show her how to make a fabric sling of sorts for carrying the child, knowing that a buggy would be problematic for the hilly paths she walked each day.

She loved the wooded mountains and the history of Hatfield Creek and could be seen at times carrying the child up into the woods or along the creek bank, singing ballads to Bess that she'd learned growing up.

> *Polly, Pretty Polly, come go along with me.*
> *Before we get married some pleasures for to see.*
> —18th Century English Ballad

She even carried Bess the mile to the Hatfield cemetery, telling tales of old Devil Anse Hatfield and the feud with the McCoys to the child, who looked blankly at the larger-than-life statue of Devil Anse. Bess was a colicky baby and Billie discovered she was calmer and happier when being carried and hearing music.

The sisters worried over Billie's devotion to the child. After all, money could only be spread so far and, to some degree, they were all dependent on Billie's largesse.

Before Bess was even a toddler, time came for another out-of-state delivery of moonshine. Billie's brothers and Arthur's kinfolk had come up with some tasty liquid which would secure big-time money in the cities. Since Billie trusted no one in the family to make these deliveries or collect the money, she was anxious about what to do about the child. Which sister could she trust to care for Bess? Helen had a child but no husband, and she drank a bit much. Pauline was too young. She decided upon Stella, the sister next to her in age, married to Andy and childless.

Seeing Billie drive up to her house, Stella breathed a deep sigh. "Here comes trouble," she told Andy who was heading out the back door.

"Where's Andy going?" Billie asked, dropping her keys onto the kitchen table.

"I have no idea and don't care," Stella poured herself a cup of coffee and asked Billie if she wanted one.

"No, but I do need a favor."

Stella stood by the window, watching Andy cross the road to the neighbor who was repairing a fence.

"You're going to have to help me out," Billie told her. "I need you to keep Bess while I'm making a delivery next week."

Helen kept looking out the window and shaking her head.

"Yes, you do," Billie told her. "Ya'll don't have no kids and having the child around might start something."

Stella didn't bother to tell Billie she didn't want no kids and she didn't like how they were conceived anyhow. She also knew Billie always got her way and she was dreading it.

"How long is this trip anyway?" Stella asked.

"As long as it takes," Billie replied, settling herself at the kitchen table and fidgeting with the salt and pepper shakers.

"What if Andy says no?" She remained with her back to Billie.

"Stella, you surprise me. You just tell him it's something you have to do, and he'd better get along with it."

Slowly turning around, accepting her fate and not wanting an argument, Stella said, "Okay, okay. Bring her on over."

Billie picked up her keys, satisfied with this arrangement, went out to her car, and waved to Andy as she headed home.

Angry with Billie and herself, Stella sat down at the table, lit a cigarette and poured herself another cup of coffee.

The trip took Billie up towards Chicago, where a local Illinois farmer sold the *shine* he bought from her and others. He liked what she brought him and made an offer for the entire load.

"Not enough," Billie told him. "This is the best *shine* you'll find this year."

They continued to discuss the cost and the farmer came very close to Billie's asking price. She knew when to stop pushing, knew that the customer had to feel he'd won something in the bargain.

The trip to Illinois was a four-day affair—two days up and two, back—and she called Stella every day to see how Bess was faring. At night, in the low-cost motel, she thought of Bess: the powdery smell of her, the softness of her pink skin and the gurgley smiles she gave freely to Billie. She missed her baby.

Stella had done her job, if grudgingly. She had kept Bess clean and fed her when she was hungry but was jealous of Andy's attention to and fondness for the child.

"Don't pick her up every time she cries," Stella had admonished him. "You'll spoil her."

"Oh, this baby needs some spoiling," he'd answer, juggling Bess on his knee. Once he'd tried to change her diaper but made a mess of it and Stella shouted at him: "Leave her alone. Keep your hands to yourself."

The first thing Billie did when she returned home was pick up Bess. Except for a diaper rash, the child appeared to have survived Billie's travels, but she seemed restless and cried more than before.

Billie continued with her businesses, sometimes travelling for a week or more as she became a person of influence in Chicago's *shine* world. Once she and her younger sister Helen made a delivery together and took five-year old Bess with them. All through her childhood Bess loved to tell stories from that time, about the lavish parties where Billie would let her tag along and carry her mother's purse. At times Bess would go to the storage closet down the hall, where the nice clothes were kept, just to see and touch the lilac silk dress she was given for the occasion. It had made her feel very special.

When left at home, Bess was parceled out to Stella or Helen. If she complained, Billie would admonish her, "Somebody's got to make some money around here. You're growing up now; you can help out with things that need to be done. We all have work to do."

Bess was growing up. She was becoming a beautiful, if sharp-featured child. Not at all like the rounded, puffy-faced women in Billie's family—sisters who noted her different appearance early on.

"Ain't she pretty," they'd remark to Billie, then give each other that puzzled look, raised eyebrows and twisted mouth. "She don't belong here," they'd whisper to each other, rolling their eyes and tsk, tsking.

When my mother Bess was about ten, Billie left for a long time. The revenuers had finally caught up with her on a *shine* run and she was sent to the new women's prison nearly a hundred miles south of Hatfield Creek for a year.

For a long time, no one bothered to explain to Bess where her mother was. She'd been left with Billie's younger sister, Helen, this time. Helen, who wouldn't explain anything, except to say, "She's away on business. She'll be back soon enough. Don't you worry." Helen may have been less strict than Stella, but she saw Bess as a housekeeper, assigning her major cooking jobs, as well as cleaning, carrying in coal for the cook stove, doing laundry. Bess hardly had a minute for herself or her homework. After two or three weeks, Bess overheard Helen talking to Stella about Alderson, the prison where Billie was incarcerated.

"They say it's a pretty nice prison. They're teaching Billie how to cook and sew. She's doing okay."

After hearing this, Bess took to her bed at Helen's. She stayed there three days, crying and running a fever, rarely getting up to eat what little food Helen managed to cook. Her mother in prison?

What had she done that was so awful they'd put her away for a year? Was her mother a bad person?

Helen became worried and wrote a letter to Billie about Bess' condition.

In a few days, Billie called Stella telling her she'd better take over; Helen couldn't handle the situation. With Billie now out of the way, Stella put her foot down, saying she couldn't handle it either. She and Andy were buying a small grocery store not far from Billie's, and there was no extra time for childcare she told Billie. Having few alternatives, Billie agreed that the child be taken to her sister Kate who lived on the tobacco farm in Virginia. She could enroll her in school there. Kate and her family had stayed behind in Virginia when the others moved to Hatfield Creek to be close to Billie and Arthur.

Billie also wrote to Bess, telling her not to worry, that she was fine and would be home before Bess even knew it. She said Bess would be going to Kate's farm in Virginia and she'd like it there. She'd have several cousins to play with.

Bess just wanted her mother to come home.

CHAPTER FOUR

Bess' Story

Bess was anxious about the move to Virginia. She was afraid of working on a farm, which she knew nothing about, and she worried her cousins wouldn't like her. As it turned out, she adjusted well to Kate's large family with both older and younger cousins around. She enjoyed the crowd and the noise and the affection they all shared. Under Kate's care she began to learn what it was like being a child and not a work horse, as she'd felt with both Stella and Helen. She loved sleeping with her girl cousins, four to a bed, all of them whispering about their day at school, whom they liked and didn't, as they fell off to sleep. Most mornings before catching the school bus, they ate a breakfast Kate had prepared: oatmeal and raspberries they grew on the farm. On the sideboard there was always a stack of bologna and cheese sandwiches for their school lunches, wrapped individually in brown paper with each child's name written on it.

She didn't even mind going with the cousins to Billie's farm to feed the cows or milk the jerseys on the weekends. She was included with their work and their play, whether cleaning up after dinner or playing Red Rover, never assigned a chore the others didn't do. She felt needed. And important.

Living among her cousins, however, she could not escape seeing how different she looked from Kate and her brood. Bess was tall and thin, with dark auburn hair and deep green eyes. Her cousins were dirty blondes with blue eyes, short and stumpy. She asked Kate about it one evening as she was undressing for bed.

"Aunt Kate, how come I don't look like my cousins? Why am I different?"

Kate hugged her for a long while. "Everybody has their own look, darlin'."

"Yes, but I don't look like anybody else I know in Mom's family. It makes me feel funny."

"You look just fine, Bess. You're a beauty, that's all." She took a deep breath and gave Bess another hug. "Now get in that bed and go to sleep."

That night Bess had a dream: Stella was arguing with Billie, saying she was tired of taking care of an orphan child and that Billie needed to send her back to China. The orphan child hid under the house so she wouldn't be sent away. Billie was looking all over for the child when Andy found her and called out, "Here she is. I've got her."

Bess shuddered when she awoke, pulled on her jumper and ran to Kate's lap.

"You okay?" Kate asked.

Bess shook her head. "Bad dreams. But I can't remember what happened."

"How 'bout I slip you some sliced apple in with your sandwich today?" She whispered.

Bess smiled and gave Kate a big hug before sitting down for her oatmeal breakfast.

Once Billie came home, things were different. She was different: stronger, somehow, and making plans for the future. She told Stella she'd learned everything she needed to know while at Alderson.

"They's nothing but women at that prison, mostly those who had to steal or rob for a living. Not bad people, just people down on their luck, trying to keep a family together. Some were *shiners* and we had good times talking about how we'd escape the revenuers. Other times we'd read magazines and play with new hairdos and makeup." Billie was glad to be home, happy to tell of her experiences at Alderson.

Stella said nothing in response to these stories, just pursed her lips and shook her head.

Billie was now out of the *shine* business, except for local deliveries. No more travelling, no more trips to Chicago. Soon enough she drove to the farm to bring Bess back to West Virginia.

Bess was reluctant. She was happy to see Billie, but at Kate's, she had felt part of a big family and dreaded being the only child in her mother's world.

"Stella and Helen make me work too hard," she cried to Kate. "Nobody helps me like they do here."

"She's your mother, honey; you have to go." Kate hugged her close.

With passage of President Roosevelt's New Deal and Work Projects Act (WPA), more people were moving into the valley, constructing public buildings and roads, cutting timber. Billie decided people needed a store where they could buy staples—bread, milk, sandwiches, cigarettes, candy—and 3% beer. West Virginia was a dry state, meaning one could only sell a watered-down beer. If you wanted something more alcoholic, you went to the ABC store, the Alcoholic Beverage Control store, which was pricey. Or you found a local moonshiner.

Billie was starting over. She knew she could sell hard stuff in the back room, under the counter, and not have to report it on Tax Day. She and Arthur had purchased several acres of Hatfield land, plenty of room for a store and maybe even some cinderblock cabins for those men who'd come for the WPA road construction. She would build living space above the store for herself and Bess and whoever else might need it.

Bess was becoming a beauty, just like her Aunt Kate had said. Dark featured, tall with curly auburn hair, a great smile.

She was in the 8th grade, happy to learn about geography and books, but she was still confused with her numbers, barely getting through each grade. She tried to get the older folks to help her with homework, but they cared little for education. One thing Bess did well was sing. And like her namesake, she loved to sing. She'd sing as she swept the floors, changed the beds, carried buckets of coal, wherever the inspiration struck.

It lifted Billie's spirits to hear her sing, thinking she must be happy to sing like that. It also brought back memories of the day she found Bess.

One day, when she was watching her mother get dressed, Bess told her, "Mom, I'm going to be in the junior high singing festival this year."

"Umm. That's good." Billie slipped the pink housedress over her head, then moved toward her bedroom. She had work on her mind: bills to pay and deliveries to be managed.

Bess followed her.

"That means I get to sing in front of the entire school!"

She sat on her mother's bed, hoping for a smile or some recognition of this important event in her life.

"Well, that's good. I'm happy for you, darlin'. Now, how're you doing with all that ironing I gave you this morning?"

Not to be deterred, Bess practiced, spending as much time as she could singing in front of the bathroom mirror, adjusting her stance, how she held her head, her hands. She had chosen a 1935 favorite "A Beautiful Lady in Blue" as her selection, having heard it on The Hit Parade. Her sultry voice fit the song and filled it with longing and disappointment.

> *Everyone loves a love story*
> *Told of a maid and a man*
> *But listen to my love story,*
> *It ended before it began.*
> —Lewis, Sam M. and Coots, J Fred, "For All We Know", 1932.

On the day of the music festival, Bess was impatient with her curly hair and the only blue dress she owned. It was a dress she'd wear to Sunday school when she could go—dark blue with small yellow flowers, a slightly curved neckline, and full skirt. She'd been reading a magazine story about women's style and make-up and wanted to look her best.

Her mother wouldn't allow her to wear make-up, but she wanted to for this occasion. She knew better than take her mother's, so she managed to steal from one of the store worker's purse the only lipstick she knew about, a Tangee Red-Red and a black pencil for drawing an eyebrow line.

I'll return it when I come home, she said to herself. It's not stealing if you return it.

No one from her family was coming to the event, which didn't surprise her. In fact, she felt more confident singing in front of people she hardly knew. On the school bus that morning, she kept going over the words of the song and crossed her fingers, hoping the upperclassman who was playing the piano for all the singers would follow her lead.

Her singing was a hit. Students who'd never noticed her came by to tell her how good she was. Especially the boys.

"I didn't know you could sing like that," a fellow classmate told her. "I like that song A Beautiful Lady in Blue too." He stood there clumsily, not looking at her directly, wanting to say more but not knowing what or how. An upper classman stood by, watching Bess' excitement with what classmates were telling her. After a few minutes, he moved forward.

"I'm Mel," he introduced himself. Bess could barely take it in as he told her he especially liked the lady in blue herself. She smiled and looked down, never having had a boy flirt with her before. She could tell he was from a good family as he was wearing a light blue dress shirt, creased khaki pants and shined shoes. Mel took her hand, squeezed it and told her he'd see her after school…

"Are you here again?" Billie wanted to give the boy a hard time. The music from the Wurlitzer forced her to raise her voice. "This is the third time you've been here, nursing a coca cola til nine at night. What's up with you, boy?"

"Just having a coke," he replied, not frightened by Billie's tone.

"Now, I know you live downtown, fifteen miles from here, and could have a coke anywhere you wanted."

"I like the company here," he smiled.

"I bet you do. You know my daughter is only thirteen and my guess is you're older. You just be careful, young man, or I'll make sure you never get up this way again." Billie nodded and gave him a half smile.

"Yes, ma'am," he told her, a big smile on his face now that Bess had come into the room.

Billie liked the boy. He was from a good family in Logan, had a part-time job during his senior year in school, and even had a driver's license. Not that Billie would allow Bess to get in the car with him.

After a few weeks, Billie decided that Bess could date no one else. Mel would be a great catch for her daughter, getting her away from the beer and *shine* and other quasi-illegal activities around the store. He was respectful and came from a good, hard-working family. When other boys came around, Billie scared them off with her aggressive tone and questions about their motives.

Once Bess was barely fifteen, Billie allowed her to go to school dances and to the movies with him, but she had to be home by nine. Bess seemed contented with the arrangement and told her mother she felt comfortable with Mel, told her he never pushed for more than a good-night kiss.

By the time she was sixteen, however, Bess wanted more. She had heard about girls at school going to third base with their boyfriends, while she and Mel never went beyond first. She was curious and wanted the experience she'd heard so much about. She started suggesting to Mel that they go all the way, but he resisted, knowing how Billie would deal with him should Bess get pregnant. Also, he held his family's values close, and knew they'd have to be married to go further. After a few weeks of pressure from Bess, however, he felt ready for that.

They made a plan to elope without discussing it with anyone, knowing the resistance they'd get from both families. Instead of a Saturday matinee, they drove to Kentucky, got married by a Justice of the Peace who charged Mel ten dollars for the wedding and fifteen for the license. Their future together was sealed. Bess was sixteen;

Mel, eighteen, a high school graduate with a part-time job.

Immediately after the ceremony, with Bess wearing her best blue dress, they stopped at a gas station to call Billie.

"Where are you? It's after nine o'clock."

"We're in Kentucky. We just got married."

"What? Are you pregnant, girl?"

"No, Mom, I'm not pregnant; just happy."

CHAPTER FIVE

A Willful Child

According to my mother Bess, I was born willful. Always wanting what I wanted, whether to be fed scrambled eggs and never fried ones, to wear this dress or that or to be left alone to read my books.

As she told it, when I was three, it was a burning summer, with humidity settling down heavy on everything that moved. I wanted an ice cream so badly I tortured her with down-on-the floor screaming tantrums until she opened the front door and screamed back, "Well, go get it then."

"Go get it," she said again, pointing to the quarter-mile curve where Johnson's Grocery claimed the only retail site in Switzer, West Virginia. "Just stay off that highway. Stay on the dirt side, Miss Priss."

I can still imagine my red, pouty, chubby face, feel the sweat on my head and the determination in my spine to get what I wanted. I walked off the porch, looking at the distant building, turning back to look home only once. Mother was standing on the front porch of our tiny white house, my colicky baby brother on her hip, flailing about.

Few cars passed on the narrow highway and when they did, dirt rose like mist and settled on the patches of wild grass and thicket on the creek side. The blacktop shimmered with heat. The hot summer had let loose a dense crop of grasshoppers, and their smell reminded me of the fireflies we'd catch on a summer evening. Grasshoppers flying among the weeds didn't come close to distracting me from my goal, but Johnson's Grocery seemed awfully far away.

I kept to the side of the road, like mother had said, kicking rocks, scuffing my patent leather shoes. The neighbors' yards were quiet, empty of children and dogs. I could hear the hum of electric fans in front of open windows. It seemed no one wanted to be out in the mid-day sun.

As I neared Johnson's, I could see an old man sweeping the dirt in front of the store, keeping things clean. He stopped, wiped his brow and nodded as I opened the screen door and went in. The ceiling fan moved hot air around in the store, where Andy Johnson was draped across the meat cooler, smoking a cigarette. No one else inside. Stella, Andy's wife and my Granny Bill's sister, came from behind the curtain that separated the store from their living quarters when she heard the bell on the screen door.

"Why, 'pon my honor! Look who's here," Stella called out. "Where's your momma? Bess isn't with you?" Stella favored my granny in looks but her dark, almost black eyes seemed scary and witchlike.

The Johnsons seemed pleased to see me. Andy tried to pick me up, but I pulled away, staying close to the check-out counter out of his reach. Stella kept saying, as she wiped the counter, "Where's your momma, little girl?" I told her she was at home. Stella looked at Andy and frowned.

Andy Johnson gave me the frozen creamsicle I wanted and asked if I'd like to sign the bill. I didn't know what he meant but shook my head no and he laughed, his extended belly bouncing as he did. Stella was on the phone, giving the operator a number to call, waving her handkerchief at me as I pushed open the screen door. "Don't you want to sit a spell, cool off?" she called out, moving her ample frame to a high stool behind the counter.

"No, thank you." I headed for home.

On the way back, I thought of nothing but the ice cream in my hand. Then, for some reason, I stopped.

I stopped and looked at the highway. I was tempted, but why?

Because it was there? Because I was free, for that moment, of my mother's requirements? Because I was angry with her? I looked to the left and I looked to the right, just like I'd been taught. I put one foot on the black top, pulled it back slowly and re-focused on my ice cream and getting home.

There she was, my mother, sitting on the steps. "You better watch your ass, little girl," she growled as she stood and held open the screen door. I said nothing and headed for the bathroom to wash the stickiness off my hands.

"You just always have to be one step over that line, don't you?" she followed. "You better start paying me some mind, or you're going to be sorry."

I went into the room I shared with my brother. He was sound asleep, and I curled up on the rug beside his crib, listening to him breathe.

I heard the phone ring and could tell it was Granny Bill because of the way my mom was talking. I heard the sharp edge in her voice as she said, "Stella had no right to be calling you. Nobody knows what a handful this child can be!"

I must have fallen asleep because the next thing I remember was the sound of Granny's voice in our living room, telling my mother to keep her voice down.

"Bess, you don't know what you're saying." Granny spoke in a loud whisper.

"There's no way you're leaving here."

"I can't stand it anymore," I heard my mother say. "My head feels like it's going to blow off. I can't do anything right. And he never helps out. He comes home and goes to that couch and sleeps until dinner." My mother's voice was high and breathless.

"He's worked hard all day, honey," Granny said. "He's entitled to some rest."

"What about me? When am I entitled to something? I feel like I'm going crazy and nobody's doing anything about it. Nobody cares what's happening to me."

I heard the screen door slam, and I scrambled off the floor, noticing Danny was still asleep.

In the living room, Granny stood near the fan, holding her skirt out to catch the cool air.

Seeing me, she said, "she'll be back, honey. Don't you worry. She'll be back."

CHAPTER SIX

Straighten Up and Fly Right

Depending on the state of my grandmother's health over the years, rumors about my mother's birth and legitimacy would rise up or fade away, with Granny Bill countering any query with "it's none of your damn business!" When Granny developed the first cancer, the gossip mill, her sisters and brothers, cranked into high gear, with her siblings fearing my mother would inherit what they felt was rightfully theirs. It wasn't that Granny had so much money: it was just that, with her various businesses, some legal, some not, she had more than anybody else in her family and they all wanted it.

My mother's interest in her origins wasn't strange at all, it fit with her lifetime insecurity and feeling that she never belonged anywhere. Even as a child, she told me once, she never felt part of Granny's extended family.

"Your grandmother was always away, working," she told me, "And I was passed around her family, staying mostly with mom's sister Stella and her husband Andy Johnson. They worked me hard. Like I was the help, not a member of the family. I never felt like I belonged anywhere, and I didn't trust Andy at all."

The loud whispers and raised eyebrows, plus the fear of Granny's imminent death, must have given my mother a courage she'd never had before, because one day she decided to find out the facts of her parenthood once and for all. I didn't witness the confrontation and couldn't hear much of it either, since I was only seven and there were two or three grownups with their ears to the door, but I'm told my mother gave as good as she got.

All I knew was, a few days later, my mother told my six-year-old brother Danny and me we were going on a road trip to North Carolina with Granny Bill. I was excited: we'd never traveled so far away before, and I had already decided I wanted to visit all the 48 states by the time I grew up. This trip would add North Carolina to the other two. Danny cried that he didn't want to go cause he always got carsick.

"You're going," my mother said, "so straighten up and fly right."

I sat on the edge of her bed that night watching as she ironed some of my best dresses and put them in the suitcase next to her own. Her mouth was tight, and I could see her jaw clench and unclench as she applied the white liquid shoe polish to Danny's shoes before putting them in a side pocket of the Samsonite bag she'd borrowed from Granny's youngest sister, Pauline. That particular car trip and the night in the motel are gone from my memory completely, but the arrival into the outskirts of Henderson, North Carolina, remains vivid.

Granny pulled the car into a short driveway that was blocked by a latched gate and cow fencing that surrounded several acres of land. Off to the right, on a slight hill, was a white Victorian house with a wraparound porch. She cut the engine and pulled out a Kleenex to wipe down the dusty dashboard.

"Now what do we do?" my mother asked nervously, tapping her ruby red fingernails on the dashboard.

"We wait," Granny said, her hands now gripping the steering wheel. "She'll see us. She'll come down."

"I suppose you worked all this out on the telephone."

"We'll just wait right here. She'll be down."

"Well, I'm not sitting in this hot car." Mother opened the door on her side, got out and leaned against the fender, shielding her eyes from the sun while looking up at the house.

"You kids get out and pick some wildflowers for the lady," my grandmother said.

"And don't get dirty," my mother threw over her shoulder.

"Who is this lady?" Danny asked.

"She's a friend of mine," was all my grandmother said.

Once out of the car, I started picking dandelions, white daisies, whatever wildflowers grew along the road, wrapping the stems in the silver gum wrapper I'd found in the driveway. Danny went around the car to stand beside mother.

Within a few minutes, a tall, dark-haired woman in a pink house dress came off the porch and started down the unpaved driveway. Granny Bill went over to the gate and nodded hello. The two of them talked for a few minutes, while Danny climbed on the wooden support of the gate and tried to get it to swing. Granny's lady friend unlatched the gate, and she and Granny walked around to where my mother had just stomped out her cigarette. I kept picking flowers, trying to ease closer and hear the conversation, when Granny said, "Bring Mrs. Carpenter the flowers you've picked for her. We're going up to the house."

Mrs. Carpenter's face was pleasant, pale against her dark auburn hair, and dominated by bright green eyes. She smiled at me as I handed her the flowers I'd picked. Entering the living room, I saw the tallest ceilings I'd ever encountered, outside of church, with lots of curved white wood around the tops of the walls and stuffed furniture arranged to face a large pipe organ with three keyboards and wooden foot pedals.

"Don't touch anything," my mother whispered as I turned a full circle looking at everything.

"Do you play, ma'am?" I asked. Handing me a glass of lemonade, she bent down as if to study me and allowed that she played for their church. "Would you play for us?" My heart was beating fast as I anticipated hearing the music.

"Leave her be, young lady," my grandmother said. "It's too hot. Now take your drink outside on the porch; you too, Danny."

Reluctantly, I took my drink out to the porch. I sat in the swing awhile, finished my lemonade, then hung over the railings and looked around. Having left my books in the car, I was bored and restless but didn't want to leave the shade of the porch. I pulled petals from the flowers that Mrs. Carpenter had laid on the wicker table to the side of the door. To the right of the house was a large field of corn, not yet tall, and, behind that, a field of tobacco. I felt comfortable, as the fields reminded me of Granny's farm. Danny was rocking and singing The Teddy Bear song he'd learned from the radio station we listened to on Saturday mornings.

It seemed an awful long time before the three grown-ups came out. "Thank Mrs. Carpenter for the lemonade," Granny Bill called out. "Now, go get in the car."

Mrs. Carpenter smiled and waved to us as we ran toward the gate, and I heard her say something about a picture. As I climbed into the back seat, I could see Granny Bill handing a Brownie camera back to her friend, who hugged my mother, then turned and went inside the house.

It was only on the ride home, as I listened to my mother and Granny talk, I learned Mrs. Hattie McCoy Carpenter, an English teacher, married to the local banker, mother of five grown children and eleven grandchildren, was also my mother's biological mother. What did that mean? It puzzled me. I'd known Granny Bill all my life. How could my mother have two mothers? I sat with my head leaning on the back of mother's seat, and listened to their soft talk. I knew not to interrupt and heard something about Mrs. Carpenter giving my mother, only a few weeks' old, away to someone who then gave her to my granny. This confused me further: I thought babies always stayed with their mothers.

Only once did my mother raise her voice. She cursed God's name and said, "Why didn't you tell me? Why did you leave me wondering all these years?"

She started to cry out loud, while Granny kept saying, "Honey, I just thought it best not to go into it. We can't change the way things are. She just wasn't able to keep you."

Part of me wanted to comfort my mother but I kept quiet. I didn't want this Mrs. Carpenter to be my grandmother and I wondered what my mother might have done to have been given away. I sat back in my seat, watched my brother sleeping peacefully, and turned my head to look for cows in the pastures or license plates from out of state, games my Granny Bill had taught me to keep from getting sick in the car.

CHAPTER SEVEN

Revelations

Twenty-four-year-old Bess had had enough.

"I can't stand being stuck in the house with two children and nothing to do," she complained to Billie. "Women are working these days. I'd go get a job if I could find someone to keep the kids."

Billie listened, not saying anything, just letting Bess say what she had to say. They were sitting on the broad porch of the old farmhouse, outside Abingdon. Billie looked out over the fields of tobacco and corn, feeling for the hundredth time how pleased she was with what her sister Kate and her family had done with the farm. She rocked slowly, then began to cough and spit into her man-sized handkerchief. She shivered as she wiped away the mucus brought about by the cancer treatment she was receiving at the hospital.

Bess leaned in, concerned about her mother. "Can I get you something? Some water?"

"No, I'm okay" Billie said, leaning back into the rocker, breathing deeply. They sat together quietly for a few moments. Bess scooted her rocker closer to her mother and reached for her hand.

"I'm fine. Stop worrying about me." She drew her hand away. Bess sighed and turned her attention to the children playing in the front yard, swinging on the tire hanging down from the old sycamore tree. She remembered the swing and the good times being there when she had lived with Kate and her cousins.

Billie had recently moved back to the Virginia farm to be closer to the University of Virginia hospital system. Diagnosed a year earlier with cancer, Billie travelled to Charlottesville every month or six weeks so she could continue the radium treatments with a doctor she liked. Even with the treatments, the doctor told her she had not much more than a year to live.

"Not me," she had told him. "I'm too mean to die."

He laughed and gave her a hug. "I hope you're right."

Bess looked over the fields in front of them, remembering how she had enjoyed being part of Kate's family and working the farm with them. She turned her attention back to her mother and saw that Billie was rocking, her eyes closed and looking peaceful. Bess sat in silence, letting her mother be.

As the evening wore on, however, with the sun setting over the barn that Billie's brother-in-law had built, Bess began to talk again about how unhappy she was at home alone with the two kids.

"Nothin' to do but keep these kids and the house clean and read magazines." Billie knew what Bess was angling for and she was going to make her work for it.

"Or maybe I could go back to school and learn something," Bess said.

"That'll be the day," Billie laughed. "A twenty-something year old being a junior in high school?"

"I don't mean public school, Mom. Maybe I could study to become a hairdresser."

"You'd be good at that." Billie looked at her daughter, smiling at her beauty while shaking her head at Bess' aspirations. This girl wants it all, she thought to herself. She's in for a peck of trouble in this life.

"Well," Billie finally said over supper that evening, "Why don't you check out one of those beautician schools; see if there's any nearby and what it might cost. I'll keep the kids as long as I can, as long as I'm feeling okay."

"Oh, would you, Mom? That would be wonderful, then I wouldn't have to worry about them."

"I'll do what I can to help, but if something comes up…."

Bess muffled Billie's response by giving her a big hug. "You are a lifesaver. You really are!"

"We'll see. You find out what you can, and we'll see."

Turns out Bess had already checked out the schools and knew there was one about seventy-five miles away in West Virginia. She could hardly wait to enroll, knowing Billie would cover the cost and keep the kids on the farm. Kate was nearby and the kids would be happy with their cousins. Bess brimmed with happiness at the expectation of this new life.

With Mel away in the army, Bess went off to Bluefield, West Virginia, to become a beautician, leaving the children with Billie on the farm. She enjoyed sharing an apartment with two other women, both of whom had husbands fighting in the war effort, their children left with their families. They went to the movies, ate at burger joints, drank in the local bars and experimented with new hairstyles and makeup. Bess had never known such freedom. She often described this period as her happiest—free of the children and my dad and able to learn a trade.

She didn't tell Mel what she was doing for a few weeks, knowing he wouldn't be happy about it. When she did write that she was attending cosmetology school, he replied with an angry letter.

Bess sat on the wicker couch in the small apartment as she opened the letter. Leaning back, she shook her head and took a deep breath. This won't be easy, she thought as she read his words.

"You belong home with our kids," he wrote. "Not running around and getting ideas about working."

As it turned out, in the months before Dad came home in 1946, Bess worked briefly as a beautician in downtown Logan, enjoying being out and sociable. Soon enough, however, her social life dried up. Billie's treatment at UVA hospital had relieved much of her pain and she was now ready to relieve Helen of her responsibilities at the store and return the kids to their mother. Bess' work life became barely manageable with these changes.

I was five when my father came home in 1946. I remember going down to the Logan train station to meet him and the excitement I felt when he came into view. He looked so handsome in his uniform. He gave my mom a big hug and kiss and then scooped me up in his arms, telling me how much I had grown since he'd left. My four-year old brother was holding onto dad's leg and jumping up and down. Two of dad's sisters were there, excited and crying, and helped us get his duffel bag into their car so that they could drive us home. As they chatted about all the changes since he'd been gone, I began to wonder what our life would be like now that he was home.

Aunt Sookie asked if he'd learned any Japanese while he was gone. He smiled and told her "Just a few choice words." They laughed together and I felt good seeing a family connection I hadn't realized I'd missed.

My father found work in the coal mines. It wasn't the work he wanted. He was bright and ambitious, eligible for the new educational opportunities offered by the G.I. Bill. But as a husband with a wife and two children and no nearby colleges, he took the work. He also put his foot down. "No wife of mine is going to have to work."

They argued for days. "I know I don't have to work, but I want to," she kept saying. "I feel better than staying home all the time."

"I can provide for us. I don't want my wife working."

In spite of her resistance and strong will, and with the pressure of work and caring for husband and kids, she bowed to the norms of the day, gave in and quit her job.

Soon enough, due to various union/mine owner conflicts and mine closings in early 1946 and '47, we left Logan for Beckley so dad could maintain a job. Beckley sat down low in a valley where the Appalachians softened toward the Blue Ridge Mountains. I don't remember moving there, as I was five-going-on-six, but it's where most of my memories start, there on a sloping hill among the working-class town folk.

During those first few months, everything was easy. My mother joined with other mothers to play cards and host Tupperware parties. My dad worked hard yet spent time with my younger brother Danny and me in the evenings. One evening, dad was helping me with my coloring, teaching me to stay in the lines and to think about whether green and purple were the best colors for the elephant. Never having seen an elephant, I argued the colors seemed just right to me. He laughingly agreed. I was inspired by the large blocks of purple and red linoleum on the living room floor where Danny would play with tinker toys or race his trucks and cars. Nearby, my mom might be making cornbread and beans or potato pancakes in the kitchen.

Dad encouraged me to practice writing my name on the lined paper he'd brought home. He showed me how to use the tiny sharpener to get the #2 pencil point just right. I was serious about learning to write my name before school started. I already knew that words had power and I bore down on pencils as if I could force words out of them.

"Take it easy. Not so much pressure," my dad would say. He'd take my hand and shake it slightly to make it relax.

"Try again." He was always gentle and patient with me. I recall a mistake I made one time and I was so mad, I nearly tore the eraser off the pencil, trying to correct it. I pressed so hard, the paper tore.

He lifted my hand and said, "Go easy. Be gentle. It'll work better that way." And it did.

I was both ready and scared to start school in the fall of 1947. Yet, I'd heard all the first graders got to color and write words and read books and then come home and eat cookies their mothers had made. I liked the whole idea. I knew I'd miss my brother, and I really knew he'd miss me.

"Sissy don't have to go to school," he'd whisper in his sweet, sad five-year old voice, day after day after day.

"But I do. It's the law."

"Mommy don't go to school."

"She's too old to go, but I have to. It'll be fun and I'll tell you everything when I come home."

"Sissy don't have to go to school," he'd repeat, following me from room to room.

I went off to school that fall, leaving my frail, cotton-headed brother crying behind me. My dad stayed home so that Mom could take me to my first-grade class. All the mothers lined up against the classroom wall and watched while their babies found chairs and crayons and friends or otherwise clung tightly to their mother's skirts as if there were a ghost in the room. My mother just looked impatient, picking at her recently painted fingernails, chatting with other mothers she knew.

The teacher's job was to coax all of us to a seat and table. As I remember it, I was cautious but easily persuaded. Some of us wanted our mothers to stay, but slowly, as we were brought into the excitement of our first day in school, we barely noticed the mothers slipping out of the room.

A teenager, I don't know who, came to pick me up at the end of the day. As we skipped down my street, I could see Danny sitting on the front steps, bouncing his bright yellow ball, waiting. The minute he saw me, he raced out of the yard, jumping up and down, "Sissy's home, Sissy's home!"

A perfect day. I couldn't wait to tell him all the things I'd learned while I was away: new words, numbers one through ten, cutting and pasting pictures. He just wanted to know if I had to go back the next day. I did and loved the whole experience. I enjoyed making new friends and learning new words and stories and drawing with multi-colored crayons. I brought my brother a new picture every day, signed by me.

Mother found a neighbor who walked her daughter Lisa to school and gladly took me along. Lisa, also a first grader, became my best friend. In December, around Christmas time, snow piled up to the window level of our house and school was closed. Danny and I both got the mumps. We were quarantined to our small, flower-papered bedroom where the white shades were pulled and where we were told if we turned on the lights, we'd go blind. In no uncertain terms, my mother told us to stay in bed and not come out.

It was breathlessly boring, and I remember sleeping a lot. When awake, Danny and I would talk about our favorite cowboys, Roy

Rogers and Red Rider, and what we hoped Santa would bring us in a few days. We loved to scoff at Hopalong Cassidy, and even Gene Autry, as the worst cowboys among them.

One night I woke up hearing my dad in the kitchen. He was whistling and making noise with the pots and pans. I looked over at Danny, three feet away in his bed, sound asleep.

I walked to the door that connected to the kitchen and called out, "Daddy!"

His voice was soft, "Get back in that bed, little girl. You're not supposed to be up."

"What are you doing?"

"Nothing that concerns you. Go on back to bed."

I punched Danny as I passed his bed and sat square in the middle of mine.

"Daddy, I smell something."

"You just stay where you are."

I could almost see him smiling, as he knew I smelled the candy cooking on the stove.

The syrupy smell of bubbling sugar and peanut butter that stole under the door into our room could only mean one thing: he was making peanut butter fudge. In my opinion, nobody else in the world could make better fudge.

"Where's mommy?" I yelled.

"Caught the bus to go to the store. She'll be back soon."

I lay down and yelled at Danny to wake up, happy in knowing what was about to happen. Soon enough, I saw the kitchen light go out and heard my dad walking toward our door.

"Don't tell your mother, now. She'll kill me if she knows I'm giving you candy at night."

"We won't, we won't," we assured him, picking out the largest square we could see or feel in the dark.

"Now, go to sleep."

"Thank you, Daddy."

Later that night, much later, a noise woke me. A quiet noise, like a cat crying. But we didn't have a cat. I looked over at Danny, sleeping. Not even a purr. Maybe a baby crying? I thought. But whose baby could it be? Did my parents have company? I slipped over to the second door in our room, the one that separated our bedroom from our parents' and listened. Again, a small cry.

Accepting that I might go blind, I put my eye to the keyhole. I could see my mother sitting at her vanity, her face in her hands, rocking back and forth. Something must have hurt her, I thought. I pushed the door open and raced to her side of the room. She pulled me close and cried for the longest time. I was shocked, I didn't know mothers cried.

"What's wrong, Mommy? Are you hurt?"

"No, no." she shook her head, wiped her eyes. "I'm not hurt, honey. Your daddy's just mad at me. Promise me that if something happens to me and your daddy, you'll stay with me."

I didn't know what she meant. What could happen? I tried to look her in the eye to ask. "Mommy, I…"

"Your daddy's mad because I got a ride home with some man I met at the store," she started crying again, "and he said he'd take you and Danny away from me if I didn't stop. Promise me you'll never leave me."

I couldn't answer. What was she saying? Why would I leave her? I felt weak from having lain in bed for so long. I burrowed my head into her shoulder. She pulled me onto her lap, rocking me back and forth, saying if I went with my dad, I'd have a mean stepmother like Cinderella. "You don't want that, do you, honey?"

I wasn't sure exactly how all this could come about, but I had the sense to know I didn't want a mean stepmother like Cinderella. I don't remember how I answered her. Or even if I did. I was out of my body, where flashing lights flooded my brain, numbing my thoughts. My heart was stilled by what she was saying.

Out of the corner of my eye, I saw my father on the front porch, flicking a cigarette toward the road and turning toward the door. I saw my own reflection in the vanity mirror, and was surprised, for

I could see but not feel my own body. "Get back to bed before he sees you. And don't say anything to your father about this. It's our secret, okay?"

I lay in my bed, wishing Danny awake, without any luck. I had no words. I just wished he would know I needed him and wake up and bring me back. Mother's secret seemed much bigger than daddy's with the candy, but I couldn't make sense of it. Daddy wouldn't leave us, what was she talking about? Somehow, finally, not hearing any more noise, I fell asleep, wondering if things would be the same tomorrow.

The next day was Christmas, and we were allowed out of the bedroom, because, they said, Santa had brought something for us. Neither parent seemed out of sorts, which made me wonder what exactly had happened in the night. It wasn't a dream, was it? Mother chided me for being so fussy and not eating the breakfast she had made. "You'd better eat if you want to see what Santa brought." No recognition of our exchange, as if nothing had happened.

Santa brought Danny a boxing set, with shiny red, padded boxing gloves and a ball attached by a flexible rod to a metal stand. Danny was so weak he could barely stand up, but he was determined to get the Joe Louis gloves on his tiny hands. I can still see his small, blond self stumble to the stand, punch the ball hard, and fall to the floor. The ball had rebounded, hitting him square in the face, giving him a bloody nose for Christmas.

My dad moved toward him, as I did, but mother pushed us both aside, pulling tissues from her apron pocket, lifting Danny's head and shouting, "I told you we shouldn't have bought this! But, no, you had to go ahead and buy it."

In that moment, I froze, not wanting to hear what she was saying. I stared at my brother, blood running from his nose, nearly covering his face. I wanted to help him but couldn't move.

"We shouldn't have bought this…?" She was saying they bought it, not Santa? What was I to believe? I ran from the room.

Up until Christmas 1947, life had seemed simple and predictable. There were the familiar arguments between my parents, of course, but, after that Christmas, things seemed more complicated. It was as if my connection to reality had loosened. How could this happen in such a short time? My mother's crying and extracting a promise from me, one that I couldn't share with my father; the possibility of having a wicked stepmother; no Santa Claus. How was it possible that my father would leave? It had never occurred to me. Things were not as they appeared, nor even as my parents had led me to believe.

I don't remember what I got for Christmas that year.

CHAPTER EIGHT

Good Girls Don't Fight

I've had two fist fights in my life. One was stopped nearly as soon as it started and is barely worth mentioning, since I was only four and the object of my rage was my three-year-old brother. I don't recall what he had done or not done, but I was mad and hit him on top of his head with my fist. Momma slapped my face and took my brother into her arms, saying, "She won't hurt you again, honey."

The second is memorable, taking place when I was about twelve and resulted in blood and tears. Oh, I'd had the typical girl vs boy fights that my friends and I would engage in from our fort high up on the forested hill behind my house. A gaggle of girls would hide, hold our breath, watching the boys try to sneak up the hill looking for us. We'd surprise them by throwing the rocks and sticks we'd stashed or by shooting rubber tipped arrows from tiny bows and yelling "Geronimo!" I'm not referring to those kinds of fights, however. I'm referring to the in your face, rip your clothes, pull your hair out kind of fight. Not the kind well-mannered girls engaged in.

This fight wasn't planned. In fact, I was sitting quietly on the school bus, returning from an uneventful day in sixth grade, resting my head on the cool metal frame of the seat in front of me. Not talking to anyone, just looking out the window at the small towns we passed through on the way to my stop at Granny's place of business, the Pioneer Inn. With the coal miners on strike and no payday, we were all back living with Granny upstairs.

As we travelled up the narrow tarmac road to where the mountains came in close, I was daydreaming and listening to the chatter noise of my schoolmates. Nothing special on my mind when I heard Elly Blankenship, two rows back, say, "At least I don't have to live above a beer garden like she does."

Without thinking, out of my seat in a flash, over the seat behind me, stepping on someone, grabbing hair with one hand and pummeling Miss Elly with the other. I don't know how I got there or what energy rush propelled me. It happened so fast it was as if something else, one of the Furies perhaps, took control of my body.

The school bus driver's shouting, "What's going on back there?" didn't stop us. Elly was shocked and her response, delayed. Her kicking only scuffed the back of the seat in front of her. We wrestled into the aisle, me on top hitting her over and over with my fist, her screaming and trying to protect her face and push me off. She finally got hold of my hair, pulled me down toward her, and I bit into the softness of her new breasts and kept throwing punches. By the time some other kids got between us, I had ripped her shirt, bloodied her nose and given her a titty bruise she'd have a hard time explaining.

"One of you get up here and sit down. Now!" The bus driver Chandler shouted and slowed down the bus. His face filled the large rear-view mirror, with him watching us and looking for a spot to pull over. Someone pushed me to the front seat of the bus. Chandler went on and on, shouting to the entire busload, about how he wouldn't tolerate this kind of behavior on his bus, and how next time he'd put us both off. Girls were giggling and whispering, and boys were whoo-hooing. Thirty-five middle school kids gone awry.

My breathing was heavy, but I saw no blood or tears in my shirt, so I settled down for the few remaining miles to my stop, feeling as if I'd had the upper hand. As I got off the bus, Elly shouted, "I'll get you for this." I shot her the finger and jumped off in front of the Pioneer Inn.

Granny Bill was drinking coffee and talking to a local at the bar, when I walked in, but, seeing my red face and ragged disposition, said, "Uh oh, here comes trouble. What's wrong, child?"

I avoided her eyes and kept walking toward the stairs that led to our rooms on the second floor. My mom came from behind the counter, followed me through the dance hall into the back kitchen where she grabbed my shoulder.

"What's happened?"

"Got into a fight on the bus."

"You what? What in hell's name…?"

"Elly Blankenship was trashing me for living over a beer garden," I answered, feeling right proud of myself. "I bloodied her nose!"

One hand on her thin hip, finger in my face, my mother raised her rooster-like voice, "Don't you know better than to pick fights? I'm ashamed of you, young lady! You've been raised better than that."

I took a deep breath, stared at the torn linoleum floor, and listened to her preach about what good people we were, how ladies don't have fist fights, and how living over Granny's beer garden was nothing to be ashamed of.

During a pause, I turned to leave, and she said sternly, "Don't you go telling your Daddy about this when he comes home either."

"Why not? I didn't do anything wrong. He'll be proud I stood up for myself."

"You know why not, Miss Priss. You know your daddy don't want us living here and this will just piss him off. He thinks living here is beneath us. He'll use it as an excuse to make us move away. So, keep your mouth shut. And I mean it!"

"All right!" I yelled, rolling my eyes and taking the steps two at a time, upstairs to where we all lived, alongside Granny Bill and two boarders who helped out downstairs. Slamming my door and falling into bed, I wiped my face with the bed sheet, cried awhile, and fell asleep. I woke up as Granny sat down on the side of my bed.

"What's wrong, honey? Tell Granny who hurt you."

"My mother, that's who."

In seconds, the world was right again as I was rocked back and forth in her soft arms, spitting out the bus story and the frustration with my mother.

"It's alright, honey, everything's going to be alright," she kept saying. And I believed her; I always believed her.

CHAPTER NINE

Piano Lessons

I stood in the doorway between the dance hall and the bar, eavesdropping on a conversation between my dad, mom, and Granny Bill at the counter. I remember that day for it was so humid in the mountains, the leaves on the maple tree outside the window were weighed down with dampness, almost as if it had rained. Nobody wanted to move. Nobody except me. They were talking about me, and it took all my will power to not to cough really loud or scuff my shoes on the old pine floors, somehow interfere with their discussion, so I could join them. If they were talking about me, I wanted in on that conversation. Yet, I knew if I interfered, they'd all clam up and I'd never find out what they were saying. I stayed put.

From what I could tell, my father was talking about piano lessons. He blew circles of cigarette smoke into the air, careful to turn away from my mom who was already annoyed with him. "Bill Rogers takes his three girls to a Mrs. White down in Black Bottom every Saturday, drops 'em off, takes his wife grocery shopping and picks 'em up on the way back home. Says the girls enjoy it." He seemed proud of himself for coming up with this idea. Mom was clearly not thrilled with him.

It was 1952 and I was eleven. We were still living above Granny's bar, the Pioneer Inn and Beer Garden, since the mine strike hadn't persuaded owners to open the mine yet and there was little money available for anything. Mom brought this up, saying, "Why spend nearly five dollars for piano lessons when we don't have a piano for her to practice on?"

"Oh, I think those church people down the road would let her practice on their piano. Johnny Greer is a deacon and lives across from the church. Comes in here on Friday nights. I can talk to him," Granny suggested.

Mom frowned, Dad shook his head in agreement with Granny, saying, "She could take the bus down to Black Bottom and catch it to come back home."

"I don't know. It's Black Bottom after all," Mom said.

I knew that could be a fly in the ointment, so I came forward. "I'm not afraid to go to Black Bottom in the daytime." The place was an African American neighborhood between where we lived and downtown where the bus terminal was located. It was always referred to as a rough neighborhood.

"You been listening to our conversation, little girl?" Granny narrowed her eyes as if to be mean.

"She'd have to walk through the mud to wherever Mrs. White lives. They don't have any sidewalks or blacktopped roads there. She'd have to get the bus back home by herself." I couldn't tell if Mom was talking to herself or my grandmother.

"Well, this child has been on the bus by herself before," Granny gave me a scrunched-up face look, reminding me of the times I had snuck on the local bus and gone to town by myself, not telling anyone.

Black Bottom was originally named for its dark, loamy soil, a great place for farmers to raise food for the family during the Depression. When the coal mines started hiring more people in the '40's, the whites left Black Bottom to live in company-owned houses and the land was bought up by negroes. In 1952 there were no streets there, just deep, black mud surrounded by two rows of houses, some on stilts, others raised up on cinder blocks to deal with the never-ending spring floods. The houses had been there since before the Depression and showed a lack of attention.

"And those niggers..." Granny said. I interrupted by lightly smacking her arm. She shook her head, "those people won't bother her 'cause they know me. Why, I been selling liquor to some of them boys for years. Anybody mess with you in Black Bottom, you tell them you're my granddaughter. They won't bother you."

Yes, she used the N word, always did except when I gave her a look or an elbow. She swore at them when they crowded the sidewalks of downtown Logan and even carried a hatpin in case one of them got too close. I never heard, however, of an actual event or experience that supported her certainty of superiority over them.

Her attitude toward blacks bothered me. She was always polite when they came to the beer garden but only served them through the back door, never allowing them in the front with the whites. This was the only fault I could find with her. Somewhere I had learned that we were all equal and had equal rights, and when I'd point out that they also had a right to half the sidewalk, she would try to shame me with, "Why, child, I thought you were smarter than that!" I never had an answer to that comment.

I didn't know many negroes but there was an old couple who came to our Freewill Baptist Church on occasional Sundays. They sat in the back pew, always nodded hello and never bothered anybody. I was always shocked that such a perfect person as my grandmother could be so wrong.

My mother poured herself half a beer and offered the remainder to my dad. "I guess we could clean house on Saturday mornings, and I could drive her to her lesson," she offered. A full minute passed before anyone said a word. My dad lit another cigarette while Granny picked up a damp rag and wiped down the counter. Finally, she said in the softest voice, "She'll be fine on the bus."

Everyone knew that giving my mother control of the car was a bigger risk than my travelling by myself, sloshing through the mud, or spending an hour alone with a negro person in her house. Just like I'd been known to sneak off on the bus from time to time, spending an hour or two at the bus station in town before returning home, my mother had a gift for disappearing. for weeks and months at a time. There was no way she was getting the car.

Her latest escapade had been in Aunt Pauline's new 1951 Chevy, when the two of them left their husbands and kids and drove to Florida to become waitresses by the beach. Just like that. I had gotten home from school one day and there was a note on her bedroom dresser, saying something like, "I'm so sorry. I just had to get away. You'll have to cook for your father. Love, Mother."

I cried and cried, partly because I didn't know how to cook. I'd already gotten somewhat used to her sudden departures. Like a stray, she'd usually return, or my father would go get her, but we all knew it was only a matter of time before she'd take off again. Giving her the car was like handing a loaded gun to a suicidal maniac.

The three adults continued to weigh the pros and cons while I stood there, now scuffing my feet on the pine floor, swollen here and there with spilled beer, and stinking of the same. Could they afford the three-dollar lessons plus the dollar for bus fare? Could I be trusted to take the bus and come back home? How concerned should they be that Mrs. White was a negro and lived in Black Bottom?

My dad shifted his shoulders, as if to lessen the tension, and spoke up, "Roberts works with me at #5 mine and says his three daughters have never had a problem."

Then, all eyes turned on me, "Would I mind having a colored music teacher? Did I want to do this, and would I practice?"

I assumed a serious face and told them it was not a problem and, of course, I'd practice. Very grown up. I wanted to jump up and shout, "No problem, folks. I am up for this!"

I heard Granny whisper to mom not to worry, that she'd pay for the lessons.

"How far does she have to go into Black Bottom?" my mom asked as both Granny and Dad walked away.

"Not far," my dad called back, "Only seven or eight houses off the main road."

They'd achieved their goal without a tantrum from my mother.

The Saturday morning I was to start lessons, I waited impatiently by the window in the bar, anticipating the bus rounding the curve. Mom told me to wear my galoshes since there was a light rain, and to be sure and take them off on the porch before going inside Mrs. White's house.

I heard her tell Stuckey, the bus driver, to watch out for me.

"So, you're going to Black Bottom for piano lessons", Stuckey smiled as he pulled onto the road. "You scared?"

"No," I told him, and he laughed. "I didn't think you would be." It was his bus I'd hide on when I wanted to slip away from home. The bus couldn't get to Black Bottom fast enough for me. I rocked back and forth in my seat, looking around to see if we passed anyone I knew, humming to myself.

As Stuckey let me off at the entrance to Black Bottom, he told me where to stand to get the bus back home. "You be careful, little girl. I'll be back before dark, about an hour and a half from now." I waved and turned to walk through the mud, glad I'd listened and worn the galoshes.

I looked around, unafraid and curious. Boys were playing basketball on the side of one house, no girls in sight. A few people sat on their porches and nodded as I passed by. One old woman called out, "You looking for Mrs. White's house?" and pointed to the well-kept two-story with dark blue siding and yellow trim toward the end of the street. I could already hear the music.

I took off the galoshes on the porch and went into the foyer in my stocking feet. No one else was there, but I could hear voices in the next room. I looked around at the photographs on the wall. Dark people, dark families, a little girl with what we called pickaninny hair braids. The photo of a negro Jesus puzzled me and made me wonder about who he really was. Was he the same person I'd read about? Just when I decided he must be a different disciple, that this was just something to make negroes feel better, Mrs. White opened the door to her parlor.

"Are you Miss Janet?" the tall, heavy-set woman asked, as she ushered a young negro boy out the door with, "See you next week." She had large breasts that seemed to be held up by a wide black belt on her dress and was what Granny would call black as a skillet. I nodded and she invited me in.

"Thank you for taking of your boots on the porch. That's quite nice of you."

"You're welcome," I mumbled, looking around at the pink, wall-papered room, inhaling the cabbage smells coming from the kitchen and wondering if I had a hole in my socks.

"I know your grandmother Billy," she offered, as I sat on the piano bench. "She's a good woman."

"Yes, ma'am," I said softly, still not sure just how she knew my grandmother.

We sat side-by-side on the bench, and she asked me questions about school and had I ever had piano lessons before.

Mrs. White's darkness was a mystery to me. As she laid her black hands over my pale ones, it was hard to concentrate, but what really intrigued me was her hair. It went every-which-way. I'd never seen hair that could stand up and stretch out like that. Once, she had me stand behind her to watch her play and I eased my left hand around to touch her hair lightly. Softer than I expected.

"Everything okay back there?" she smiled at me. I nodded and she kept on playing, a wide grin on her face. "Okay, now watch my hands as I play."

There were so many questions I wanted to ask her: did she really think Jesus wasn't white? What made her hair that way? Could the color of her skin rub off on me? Did she think I could be a star? I held my tongue, knowing I was not to be rude to older people, no matter what.

That day we covered the notes E G B D F, and she reinforced them by saying, every good boy does fine. Somehow, I learned to play "Row, Row, Row your boat" and I knew I'd be a star!

I couldn't wait to tell Stuckey about how different the house smelled and about the black Jesus and Mrs. White's soft hair. He just smiled and nodded and said he was happy for me. For the next two weeks, I went to the Freewill Baptist Church twice a week to practice the lessons Mrs. White had given me. I even tried to pick out notes from the hymnal but wasn't good at it.

Coming home from practice one afternoon, I was greeted at the screen door by Maggie, a middle-aged woman who worked for Granny behind the bar counter. "Come see what your Granny got you today."

Granny was sitting on the barstool talking to some man who looked familiar when I came through the door. "That delivery truck outside must be his," I thought.

She told me to put my music book behind the bar and come wash off the counter where the two were sitting. I did as I was told, looking around the bar area to see if I could find some surprise from her. Nothing I could see, just the same gallon jars of pickled pigs' feet and hard-boiled eggs on the counter. Half-full ash trays. Empty beer bottles. Nothing beside the cash register except papers from the bread delivery man. I wandered over to the Wurlitzer, thinking maybe she'd gotten new records on it that day. Nothing here either, just Patsy Cline, Hank Williams and the Tennessee Mountain Boys. I checked to see if maybe the juke box man had been here and left me some free plays on the Wurlitzer, but no. It still required a nickel a song or three for a dime.

Granny kept talking to the man, with long lapses between their words. I knew better than to interrupt her, especially to ask if she'd gotten me a present or something. That kind of question never got a straight answer. I'd usually get, "Now why would you think I'd get you a present, smarty pants?"

I ambled over from the jukebox to where she sat on the stool, leaned my head on her shoulder, eased my way between her legs until she half lifted me to her lap, and I breathed in the sweet smell of Pond's Cold Cream.

"What do you want, child?"

"Nothin'."

"Then why are you getting all over me when I'm having a conversation?"

"Maggie said you had something for me."

"She did? Well, I'm going to have to get after her for that."

She made a move to get off the stool. I stood firm.

"Granny, do you have something for me? Maggie said you did."

"I don't know what she was talking about." She moved behind the counter. The man waved goodbye and left the bar.

"Granny, I know you do. I can tell from your face. What is it?"

"Lord, would you listen to this child! Stop carrying on and go into the dance hall and bring the salt and pepper shakers in here to fill up."

"Granny!"

"Go on now. Do what I tell you."

The dance hall was dimly lit by another Wurlitzer and two deep set windows on either side. I went from booth to booth, collecting as many salt and pepper shakers as I could hold against my chest and moved toward the kitchen. That's when the shakers hit the floor.

"Granny," I screamed. In the corner, next to half a dozen boxes of empty beer bottles, was an upright piano that seemed to be on its last legs. There was no stool, so I grabbed a beer box, turned it on its end and pulled it close. I was torn between hitting every key as loud as I could or playing the one song I'd learned. Granny and Maggie stood in the door of the dance hall entrance, smiling, yelling for my mother to come see.

I leaned into "Heart and Soul" with two fingers. The piano hadn't been tuned but the music never sounded better to my ears.

CHAPTER TEN

The Rose Room
1953, Granny's Farm

"Let's go in here and talk," she said, guiding my shoulder toward her bedroom. Granny Bill closed the door and sat on the small stool that fronted her oversized maple dresser. She fidgeted with her hand mirror and comb while I looked around, not knowing whether to sit or stand. The wall-papered room was small, barely enough room for the bed, the maple dresser and a narrow chest of drawer. I settled on a sunny spot on the floor, across from her bed. The three-paneled mirror on the dresser reflected her softness from every side.

"They's some things we need to talk about that are not easy. You understand?" She bent down to look me in the eye. I shrugged, "I guess so." I could tell this was going to be a grown-up conversation, difficult for a twelve-year-old. "Now, your daddy's a good man, Janet. Sometimes he don't act like it, but he means well, you know?"

I nodded, agreeing with her, even though from an early age, there was a strangeness to my parents. They weren't like my friends' parents, with my mother disappearing every so often and my dad somehow persuading or coercing her back to the family after a few months.

We'd adjust, she'd rearrange the all the furniture, and then be off again.

This time, as soon as my dad left West Virginia for Tampa, Florida to work for a friend of his, a necessity while the mines were closed, mom left in a flash with her aunt Pauline. They headed for West Palm Beach and what they considered the good life, taking jobs as waitresses in a steakhouse near the beach. Nobody needing her or telling her what to do. She left Danny and me behind with Granny and with strict instructions not to say a word to dad about her whereabouts. I was trying to remember how long she'd been gone when Granny pulled at my shirt.

"Are you listening to me, girl? He's a good man but his coming in and taking you and Danny out of school today… well… that wasn't right," she hesitated.

In the silence, I waited, studying a filmy rainbow on the wall, and following it to its source, the light bouncing off the metal strip of her pine handkerchief box and spreading across the big pink roses on the wall. I always thought of her bedroom as The Rose Room because of the wallpaper and the roses on the linoleum. Today, the room smelled of Pond's cold cream and my own sweat.

Earlier today, my classroom smelled of sweet lilac. I sat there, with the other sixth graders, trying to pay attention to the geography lesson about North and South America, but I was daydreaming and inhaling the lilacs blooming outside the half-open window.

"There ain't nothing sweeter than lilacs and peonies," Granny would often say. Then we'd laugh and both of us claim, "Except for you!" We'd chase each other to give love pinches that always ended in hugs and kisses and giggles.

North and South America got dropped like a hot potato when my father walked into the classroom today. His sudden appearance startled even the world map that was pulled down over the black board and it seemed to wave him by. He stood at the edge of a row of wooden desks, looking down each one till he found me.

"Janet, get your books and come with me."

Mrs. Mercer tried to say something, but he cut her off, "She won't be back."

My surprise was stung with fear and excitement at seeing him after so many months.

Somebody must be bad sick, for him to be here, I thought to myself and hurriedly pulled the books and papers out of my desk, carefully folding my book report down the middle the way Mrs. Mercer liked. She looked at me questioningly as I handed it to her. I didn't know what to say. My best friend Barbara mouthed "I'll see you later," and I nodded, not knowing what to expect.

Danny was waiting in the hallway, trying to balance his books, his Superman lunch box and his baseball bat in his thin eleven-year-old arms. He gave me a confused look and I just shrugged. Dad wasn't saying anything except, "Get in the car."

I tried to find out where we were going and what was happening, but dad wouldn't answer me. He was quiet on the entire drive to the farm, saying only, "We'll talk about all this when we get home."

Danny had a strained look on his face but remained quiet in the back seat next to me, looking out the window. My mouth tasted like I'd sucked on a piece of metal, and swallowing a lot wasn't helping. I wondered if someone had died. But I thought he would have said so if that were true. I couldn't make sense of what was happening, and I was getting more nervous by the mile.

I hugged my books to my chest as if they would keep me from floating away. Danny sat close, rocking from side to side. As we approached the farm, dad stopped to let us off by the springhouse. "Go start packing," he told us. "Tell your granny I'll be right back, I'm going for cigarettes."

Back in the Rose Room Granny cleared her throat, raked her fingers over her knees and took a deep breath, "What I'm trying to say is, you know how your momma and daddy argue all the time, and your daddy had to go work in Florida when the mines closed earlier this year?" The words rushed out before she could call them back. She pulled at the bodice of her house dress and seemed to be searching for more words. I had a spasm of courage and turned to her.

"Well, yes, but nobody ever explained why mom and Aunt Pauline went to Florida in the first place... the whole other side of the state from where he was. Nobody ever explained that to me." I locked my fingers into a steeple and flushed, fearing my words had sounded harsh.

"Honey, that's what I'm trying to tell you."

"What?"

"Your daddy found out that your mother and Pauline was down there waitressing. Somebody told him, I still don't know who. Anyway, he's mad at me for sending your mother's letters to him, the way I did, you know, in that other envelope." She pulled a handkerchief from her buxom, wiped at a dusting of face powder on the dresser, and then used it to pat her neck dry. She avoided looking at me.

"And?" The facts were making me dizzy and impatient.

"And, so, he's taking you and Danny away, down to Florida with him. He says you all are leaving tomorrow morning." She covered her eyes with her hand, as if these words were too much for her. "I'm sorry, honey; I'm so sorry. You know how your mother can be when she sets her mind to something. I didn't know what else to do when she told me she was leaving."

I knew this letter business had been going on, but nobody ever explained anything. Granny would get a letter from my mother, and there'd be a special envelope in it, addressed to my dad, and Granny would put it out for the mailman. When I'd ask, Granny would just say, "It's for me to know and you to find out, little girl!"

Sometimes there was a letter in the envelope for Danny and me and, sometimes, two crisp one-dollar bills. Granny's "tsk tsking" at this always made me think she disapproved of children having that much money. It was only later I understood her displeasure with my mother on all fronts.

I sat there, now, knees up against my chest, more confused than ever, inhaling my own sweat and trying to cross my toes over one another. I didn't know what to say. I just rocked back and forth and crossed my toes.

Granny stood up, "You're gonna have to go with him, honey. He's your daddy. And…" she pulled her soft pink dress away from where it had lodged in the crevices of her body, "We have so much to do to get ready! Let's get going, girl!"

As the tears welled up, I opened my eyes wide, trying to stretch my face so they wouldn't fall. It wasn't that I couldn't cry in front of her; I just didn't want to cry over this.

"I'm not going," I coughed. "I'm staying here."

She pulled me to her, "Oh, honey, I'm so sorry. I wish that daughter of mine would grow up. She's hurt you children terribly."

The tears raced down my sunburned face leaving salt lines in their path. "I'm not going," I said. "I'm staying with you."

"Child, I wish you could. I wish you could. But he's your daddy and he's made up his mind and… uh oh, here he is, driving up the hill." She shook me softly and wiped my face with her handkerchief. "Go wash up. Don't let him see you this way."

I ran out the back door of the house, past Danny who was eating Saltines and grape jelly on the side porch and ran further up the hill to my favorite spot. From the limestone rock where I often lay and studied the stars at night, where I dreamed about boys and the future, I could see my dad walk up on the porch, flick his cigarette away from the house and go inside. I couldn't tell if he'd said anything to my brother or not.

How can I explain what I felt? Fear? Confusion? Hurt? More like dread. More like waiting for the other shoe to drop. How could Granny not fight for me? Here was my father, whom I hadn't seen in months, and he was like a stranger to me, demanding I leave the place where I felt safe and protected. He wanted to take us from granny's where I slept peacefully and woke up to hear her talking about the farm chores of the day and where I knew what was expected of me. Here he was, wanting to drive all the way from Virginia to south Florida to confront my mother with her tricks and lies. God knows she was full of them, more than he even suspected.

I thought about the times a few years earlier when I was about seven. She'd wake me at night, asking if I'd like an ice cream, and we'd end up at some beer joint down the road.

Me, half asleep in my pajamas in the corner booth; her, drinking beer and dancing with some man. "Now, if your daddy wakes up when we get home, you tell him you wanted an ice cream," she would say.

Right, I thought. More secrets and lies. Even a second grader would know that no parent in her right mind would get up and go out in the middle of the night, drive ten or fifteen miles, to satisfy a child's desire for ice cream.

No, I definitely didn't want to be part of the arguing and accusations that would occur between the two of them when they met up in Florida. Somehow, I always ended up the middle of their arguments. He said… she said… well, Janet said… and Janet knew about it… and, why'd you tell Janet and not me?

Why didn't he just go talk to her himself once he found out where she was? Why did he have to drive all the way up here, get us and throw us in her face? Their business was their business. I wondered about these things and slowly admitted to myself, I knew why. It gave him the upper hand, having my brother and me in tow. He'd get her back. One more time, he'd get her back.

"Oh, God, why can't they leave me out of it!" I said out loud, wondering how I could escape them? Where could I go, if Granny insisted I leave with him? Why couldn't she stand up for me? I knew the answer to this question as well; I just didn't want to admit it. Because they were my parents, not her. She had no rights. Reluctantly, exhaling a deep breath, I admitted I had no place else to go. My back ached from leaning into the cold rock and I stood to stretch.

"Janet, come help me with dinner," I could see my grandmother calling from the porch.

"Come on down, now. We have to eat. Your daddy's hungry."

There was no way out. If I ran away, they'd find me, and I'd be in bigger trouble.

Reluctantly, I walked down to the house. Dad sat at the table with Danny, telling him what to write down on the tablet in front of him. He motioned for me to sit and slid a sheet of lined paper to me.

"I want you to write your mother a letter. Tell her how awful she is for deserting you and Danny. We'll give her the letters when we get there."

Deserted? I didn't feel I'd been deserted. I loved living with my grandmother. I felt safe and happy. I protested, "Why are you making us do this? I don't want to write a letter!"

"Sit down and write the letter," he said sternly.

I slammed my fist on the table, "I don't want to go!"

"You're going," he said, "So sit down and write the letter."

There was no place to run, no place to hide. Granny busied herself at the stove, looking over and shaking her head sadly.

I don't know what I wrote. I took a deep breath and pushed my feelings down to hide my helplessness and the feeling of being used like a puppet. I would go with my dad, but I could never trust either of my parents again. And Granny? Well, that was another story altogether.

CHAPTER ELEVEN

Dancing in the Dark

Setting: Day room of clinical memory facility
Characters:
Maggie–the group worker/facilitator
Two mu'mu's–Edna and Ellen
Arlene–teased black hair with blue hydrangea in it
Lavender–remote, intellectual

Maggie dragged her chair from the foyer into the dayroom of the clinical facility, noticing that the four women assigned to her were already sitting in a circle near the jukebox. Except for Edna who leaned into the Wurlitzer, moving side to side to Frank Sinatra's version of "Dancing in the Dark." The bubbling neon lights from the jukebox shaded Edna's paper-white legs to a lovely pink, then green, then blue. She knew that Edna had been a singer in her day, mostly in run-down clubs on Appalachian backroads, that she loved music and she had a big crush on Frank Sinatra.

Dancing in the dark 'til the tune ends
We're waltzing in the wonder of why we're here
Time hurries by, we're here and we're gone
—Dietz, Howard, and Schwartz, Arthur. "Dancing in the Dark". [Recorded by F. Sinatra], Harms, 1931.

As the song ended, Edna returned to her seat between Ellen and Lavender. Lavender pulled her chair away from the circle, frowning as if dissatisfied.

"What's the matter, Lav," Maggie asked. "You don't feel like talking today?" Maggie handed her a Styrofoam cup of coffee, "lots of cream, just how you like it."

"I'm just thinking," Lav responded and turned her chair sideways to the small group.

"Well, don't get lost now," Maggie frowned at her.

Looking bright and cheerful in her tight, yellow, matching Bermuda shorts and tank top, her large arms hanging out like a stuffed sock from the sleeve area, Maggie stomped the floor with both feet. "OK, girls, let's get focused. Yesterday we were talking about our favorite movies and movie stars. Does anyone want to pick up our conversation from there or do you want to talk about something else?"

The two women in mu-mu's, Edna and Ellen, kept talking to each other but looking elsewhere.

"Edna, we're getting the group started," Maggie whispered loudly and the two quieted down. No one responded to Maggie's question for a full minute during which time Arlene, all in black with a large blue hydrangea pinned to her dyed black, teased hair, crossed her legs and began to rock back and forth in her chair.

Ellen whispered to Edna. "She's on new drugs today. Watch out!"

Edna, who was next to Lavender on her right, was making sculptures with her hands, talking quietly to herself, not listening to Ellen: "This is the church; here is the steeple. Turn it around and HERE ARE THE PEOPLE!" The last of her outburst surprised everyone in the group, making Arlene rock faster in her forward and backward movements.

"Oh, you want to talk about people?" Maggie suggested, "What kind of people?" She was starting to sweat, both with the heat in the room and the frustration of getting this group to talk about their day, their fantasies, their feelings… anything that would help them focus, give them some confidence, anything to help them get through the day.

No one responded to Maggie's invitation. Maggie pulled her mostly gray hair back from her face as if to make a ponytail. This is killing me, she thought. If I weren't so old, I'd get a different job.

"Well, I'll talk about people, and you can join in," she told the group.

"Hmm," she started: "I could tell you about a wonderful woman I used to work for. She lived in the mountains of Appalachia and was a very successful bootlegger."

"Hah!" Lavender laughed and moved her chair back into the circle. "This'll be good!"

"She was quite a lady and she treated me real good." Maggie smiled. She became quiet for a moment, musing about the time she worked at Billy's beer garden and lived in one of the cinderblock cabins out back.

"I've told you about her before, so maybe this time I think I'll tell you about my former husband, Bob."

"I have a husband," said Edna. "He travels with Frank Sinatra."

"That's good, that's good. Well, my husband Bob had been a coal miner; he was a good-looking man but nearly blind from the dust underground. He was on disability when I married him, and I didn't have a dime to my name. He could get around but not do much."

Maggie looked around the circle of middle-aged women, hoping to see a light of connection to her story telling.

"That woman I told you about hired me to work the bar, and gave me my own room, but made Bob live upstairs over the business." Maggie clasped her hands, as if in prayer, but really because she enjoyed reminiscing.

"After a few months, I didn't want anything more to do with him, but he had no place to go. So, Billie gave him a little work, sweeping up, carrying out the empty beer bottles and setting up the cooler. But, Lord, he had the stinkiest feet in the world! Worse than a skunk or even a dirty toilet!" Maggie bent over, her head touching her knees, laughing softly.

"Whew! Billie did all she could to help him, buying him powders and things to put in his shoes but nothing worked. You could smell him before he entered a room," Maggie laughed louder and shook her head as if to rid herself of the scent.

"Sometimes, if Billie had a crowd at the bar, she'd tell him to leave the room!" Maggie pulled a blue bandana from her back pocket.

"One day I told him our marriage was over because he made me nauseous!" She bent over with laughter, raw and guttural snorts and nearly choked on her own saliva.

"I'm fine, I'm fine," she said, wiping her mouth with the blue bandana.

"Alright now, anybody else want to talk? Have you ever met anyone like Bob?"

She hoped she'd provoked some reaction, but the women stared back at her, as if confused by what she'd been saying.

Ellen stood up and said, "I saw a movie one time where there were lots of people dancing. They wore such pretty shoes!" She began to waltz toward the center of the group, her eyes half-closed as if she could hear the orchestra, see the other dancers.

"Enzio Pinza!" shouted Lavender. "He was the one in that movie we saw last week. He's the one."

"He was not," shouted Edna, "It was Clark Gable!"

"What movie?" Arlene asked Lavender, who paid her no attention.

Maggie got up and tried to get mu-mu Ellen back to her seat, but she held onto Maggie's hand and tried to dance with her.

"South Bronx or Pacific Ocean or something like that." Lavender turned her chair around and looked at the ceiling. Pointing to her temple, "I knew the answer was in there somewhere. I just knew it."

Mu-Mu Ellen sat down, whispered something to Edna, and the two giggled, hands over their mouths—like twins in a circus show, thought Maggie, taking a deep breath.

"Good thinking, Lav," Maggie smiled, not mentioning that Enzio Pinza was not the actor in the film they'd seen. "Good work."

"I know a lot of things," Lavender responded with a smile. "It's all in here," she knocked on her head.

"I thought we were talking about people," Arlene whined. "I wanted to talk about people. Nice people."

"Has someone been nice to you this week, Arlene?" Maggie asked as she settled back in her chair.

"Um, I think so. Oh, yes! Yes!" Arlene clapped her hands. "It was that man who cleans the floors. He told me I should be careful, that the floors were very wet."

Maggie smiled, "That was very nice of him to warn you about the wet floor."

"Nooo. He wasn't warning me. He was nice."

"He winked at me the other day," Ellen offered. "I ran away down the hall."

"That hall needs to be cleaned more often," Lavender whispered loudly. "Sometimes I find dirty Kleenexes and bobby pins on the floor when I walk down to dinner. Disgusting!"

"Would you like to speak to the administrator about that, Lav?" Maggie asked. "You can; it's perfectly okay to do so." Lav turned her chair sideways to the group again. "Nope. Not me, not me."

Maggie looked at the group and let out a deep sigh: "Our time is about up, girls. Is there anything else you want to talk about today?"

"I want to dance," Edna said, and took mu-mu Ellen's hand. They began to move slowly around the group meeting room, humming the Happy Birthday song together.

"Oh, what a good idea," Arlene squealed. "Let's dance!"

Arlene invited Lavender to join her, which she did.

I've had zero luck with this group today, Maggie thought.

Maggie danced by herself, smiling as the women began to move around the room. Lord, I did all I could do with this group today, she prayed silently. Please make it better tomorrow.

A staff member in the hallway passed the room, stepped back to look at the group. She shrugged her shoulders. "What's going on in there?" she asked the custodian. "It's some kind of dance class, I think," he said, as he continued mopping the hall.

CHAPTER TWELVE

A Day in the Life

Pauline couldn't get the hymn out of her head. It was stuck like a needle on an old record. Over and over she hummed and sang the words she remembered from her girlhood, church-going days. "Amazing Grace" was one of the altar calling hymns she'd learned as a child.

Amazing grace, how sweet the sound.

Pauline turned on the ignition of her '55 Chevy Bel Air on the dark, back street of downtown Logan, West Virginia. She sat for a while, ignoring the honking of car horns around her, humming the song to herself. She needed to make up her mind whether to go home or go on up to Mountain View. There was a bar and a hillbilly band on Friday nights at the Mountain View Inn, and her friend Rita had said she'd meet her there. Tired from her shift at Morrison's Drive Inn, what Pauline really wanted was to take a long bath and rid herself of the chili dog and sauerkraut smells she'd absorbed during the day. She just wanted a whiskey and seven-up but not at home by herself.

She'd stayed in town after her shift. Another job interview. The drugstore on Peekin' Place had an opening for a waitress at their soda and sandwich bar. Tired of the in-and-out business at Morrison's Drive Inn—dripping sweat in summer and teeth-chattering cold in winter—Pauline wanted someplace normal. Peekin' Place Drugs wasn't exactly that, if you counted what went on upstairs, but at least she'd be inside and able to have a cigarette in the back room from time to time.

Pauline had known the owner, Bob Blankenship, for several years—he had once owned a supermarket near downtown—and she thought he wouldn't pressure her to work for extra money upstairs. The downstairs was normal looking, with just the soda fountain and the pharmacy. Folks came in the back door if they wanted the services upstairs.

Bob had pretty much told her she had the job, saying she'd need to have her own uniforms and that Friday was their busiest day. Pauline said she could start on Monday, and he nodded.

As she sat in the car deciding where she wanted to go, Pauline saw Ed Whitman, an old boyfriend, come into view. He pounded on the hood of her car and asked if she wanted a beer. Said he was heading to the Red Top Club. Sounded good to her. At least they had a jukebox there. She turned off the ignition.

Ed hadn't changed in all the years she'd known him: big flirt, full of bluster, not to be trusted, but full of fun. They sat at the small round table in a dark corner with Pauline laughing and pushing away Ed's hands when they found their way to her leg, shaking her head at his stories. They were on their second beer when his wife walked in. Before Pauline knew what was happening, Eula was slamming Ed over the head with her shellacked basket purse, yelling "son-of-a-bitch" and "I told you…."

Pauline eased out of her seat and headed for the door, laughing all the way.

"Damn, you know he deserves everything that woman delivers!" She shouted to the other customers, many of them familiar faces, who were thumping the tables and hooting at a scene they'd witnessed before.

Outside it was dark and foggy. Pauline realized her car was a short piece down the road and she felt a strong need to relieve herself. I'm not going back in there, she thought as she looked around.

Shoot. If I go up that way to Mountain View tonight, I'll never get past Billie's place. I'd have to stop and say hello. she was talking to herself now. She was right. If someone saw her and it got around she hadn't stopped at her sister Billie's, there'd be hell to pay. "I want something new," she shouted out to the empty street.

She then murmured, "I already know all those old drunks who hang out at Billie's on a Friday night. I don't need that." She realized the bus terminal was just across the street. That's good, she thought, crossing the street and willing herself not to let her bladder go loose.

Time had gotten away from her today. She hadn't meant to work all day, but Myrtle called in sick and the boss asked her to stay until seven. That delayed her meeting with Blankenship, but she had gotten the job and, even though she was tired, she now wanted to celebrate.

She walked between two Greyhound busses toward the inside. Spying one of the regular bus drivers at the curb, she waved.

"Hey Honey, you going on my bus tonight?" he offered in a friendly voice.

"No, just going to visit the lady's room."

The driver gave her a big smile and said, "Well, we have a bathroom in the back of the bus!"

"Nope. Not tonight." She waved again before going inside and entering the smelly restroom.

Inside the stall, she squatted and relieved herself over the not-so-clean toilet. Damn. No toilet paper. Shake, shake, shake!

As she tried to wash her hands at the crusty sink, she cursed the dribble of water, the empty soap container and, finally, the lack of paper towels. She studied her face in the mirror and winced at how tired she looked. She wiped her wet hands on the backside of her uniform and opened the door to the bus station's waiting room.

"Ya'll need some paper in there," she shouted across the room to the man behind the ticket counter.

"See you, darlin'," he yelled and waved as she crossed toward the door.

"Damned idiot," she cursed under her breath and pulled her cardigan closer.

Here she was in downtown Logan, 9:30 at night, with at least three routes out of town.

Hmmm, she said to herself, I don't want to go home, up to Omar, but I might could drive on up past the house and head up to Mountain View, sneak past Billie's place. She hurried to her car.

Pauline settled in her messy car, shoving newspapers, paper cups and straws onto the passenger side floor. She leaned back in the seat, closing her eyes. That song again: *Amazing Grace* was embedded in her slightly tipsy brain tonight. She turned on the radio. The radio soothed her and brought tears to her eyes at the same time: now the Platters were singing *The Great Pretender* which made her think of Ivan, who was at present driving his wife to her people in Tennessee.

"Ain't no way around it," he'd told her. "Effie don't drive and Gene's too young to drive that far."

"Put her on a friggin' bus!" Pauline had told him, but he just shrugged and left the room.

Ivan. So many years they'd been together, good ones, like when Gene, their son, was born fourteen years ago, and bad ones. When things were bad—when Pauline was angry or demanding or drinking too much—he'd always go back to Effie's. Then he'd be back, as if nothing had happened.

"What are you doing here?" she once asked him after a two-week separation.

"Do you want me to go?" he'd responded. No, she didn't. She never did, in spite of his refusal to get a divorce. "Effie is family," Ivan would say. "I've known her for forty years."

Ivan, a local boy born and raised in Logan County, was a coal miner like most other men in that part of the state. A high-school education at best. He was cute, five feet tall, skinny and blonde, never short of a plug of Mail Pouch in his jaw, which cut the cuteness for most women. Not Pauline.

She was in her mid-twenties when they met, tall and curvy, unmarried and wild as swamp milkweed. "Sowing her oats," said her half-sister, Billie. "That girl will never slow down."

But she did. No one understood the attraction between her and Ivan, but it was as obvious as sunlight. "I just feel something when I'm around him," she'd explain. "That's it."

Everyone knew he was married, but it didn't make any difference. Ivan and Pauline, soap and water, beans and cornbread. They went together.

Pauline shifted in her seat and turned the volume on the radio down.

She had always been a hard worker, mostly as a waitress at one drive-in or another about the county. Once she found a run-down piece of property in Chauncey, on Island Creek, and she asked her half-sister Billie for help to open a beer joint. Billie drove down to look and saw that the place was on a large muddy flat with a few dozen coal camp houses around and two bridges off the main road: one, a car bridge of railroad ties, the other, a swinging bridge that folks without a car could walk over.

"Well, I don't know how you can make a run of it," Billie told her as she wrote the $500 check for Pauline's down payment. "I'll help all I can, but you've got a pile of work ahead of you." The first thing Pauline did was scan the Logan Banner classifieds for a used oven, a coal stove and a second-hand mattress.

Business was slow, very slow. Old run-down, injured coal miners would come in to nurse a bottle of beer for hours on end, occasionally joined by their drinking friends who did the same. Occasionally someone would put a quarter in the juke box to hear Hank Williams or Kitty Wells. One man, Ernie Swagger, always stayed until she threw him out. "Go on home," she'd say, paying no attention to his muttering and hunched over procession to the door. One night, she asked Ernie where he lived.

"Oh, wherever I can," he slurred. "Sometimes with my daughter, sometimes in that shed down by the bridge. I ain't got no home."

Pauline asked around and discovered that two or three other drinkers were in the same situation, just drawing the tiniest of social security or company insurance. It gave her an idea for making more money.

"How much life insurance you got?" she asked Ernie one evening. "About two thousand dollars now," he offered.

Pauline smiled. "How about you sign over that insurance to me, and keep your social security for spending money," she said. "I'll give you a room in the back where you can stay. I'll even throw in one meal a day. I've got plenty of room back there." Ernie gave her a toothless smile.

Why am I thinking of those old days? Lord, I barely survived those two years in business, Pauline shook her head and started her car just as it began to rain. "Well, that's a bitch," she said aloud as she pulled onto the two-lane road and turned up the radio. Johnny Cash was singing *"I Walk the Line."*

As she approached the turn that would take her toward home, she saw a young girl hitchhiking by the traffic light. Lord, what is she doing out in this weather? Pauline wondered and slowed down.

"Where you going?" she yelled out the window.

"Up near Omar," the girl responded and shifted her heavy load of gear as she moved toward the car.

"Well, get in back then."

"What's your name, honey? What are you doing out here hitching a ride? Don't you know it could be dangerous?" Pauline turned on the wipers.

"Didn't have no choice. Have to get this baby home."

"What! You got a baby under that coat? Jesus Christ!" She turned to look, only to be shocked by the deafening horn of a passing car. "How old?"

"Jesse's not quite a year old. My dad threw us out of his house tonight. Said the baby was too noisy and too much of a bother. I'm going up to my sister's house to stay." The girl adjusted the blanket around the baby.

Pauline sighed. The trouble some people have! she thought. Poor girl looks like she's about fifteen herself and here she has a baby and no home.

"She taking you in?" Pauline asked.

"She don't know it, but she is."

Pauline shook her head and reached for her pocketbook.

"Well, honey, you've got yourself quite a mess. You got any money?"

"I can give you a dollar for gas," the girl replied.

"No, not for me. You telling me you only got a dollar to your name? What the hell?"

"I'll be alright," she replied and put the whimpering baby on her shoulder, whispering low and patting the child on the back.

Pauline drove slowly in the rain. Fog was coming in, making it difficult to see.

"What's your name, sweetheart?"

"Jody. But everyone calls me Sister."

"Jody what?"

"Blankenship. I'm Bob Blankenship's daughter."

God help me! Pauline reached for her wallet. Here I am with my new boss' daughter that he's thrown out of his house. Why me, Lord?

"You know him?" Sister asks.

"Sort of," Pauline replies, trying to anticipate how things might go in the near future. She was quiet for several minutes. Sister was humming a tune, rocking the baby back and forth.

"Where's the baby's daddy?" she asked, looking at the girl through the rear-view mirror.

"Oh, he's around some. I heard he took a mining job over in Williamson, but I haven't heard from him for some time."

Pauline shook her head. It gets worse by the minute, she thought. Both were quiet for several miles. The girl kept humming to the baby and looking out her window.

"Where do you live?" the girl broke the silence.

"Just another mile or so up the road, next to the Gulf service station. Where can I let you out?"

"Slow down up here by the yellow house. My sister lives out that road."

"I'll drive you to the door."

Pauline maneuvered the car onto the narrow dirt road, fronted by small shotgun houses. Sister pointed at a small white house with car parts in the yard. "This is it."

She got out of the back seat, shuffled the child onto her other shoulder, and Pauline handed her the singles she'd found in her purse.

"Are you sure you're alright? Do you want me to wait?"

"No. We'll be fine here."

Pauline watched the girl climb the stairs and knock on the door. Figuring she was okay, Pauline backed out the dark road to the highway and headed home.

This is too much. I'm going home, fixin' myself a drink or two and climbing into the tub. No night life for me tonight.

Gene, her son, was sound asleep in his room, offering a soft snore as a welcome sound as Pauline opened the door. Good to be home, she thought. Her kitchen, neat as a pin, was comforting. She reached for the metal ice tray, took it to the sink, opened it, dropped a couple cubes in the tall glass and poured a healthy shot of Four Roses. She drank the whole thing before pouring a second, still standing at the sink. "Whew," she said out loud. "I feel better already."

Sliding into the hot bath water, Pauline leaned back and took a long draw of her second drink. Yes, it's good to be home, she said to herself. She thought about her day: full of surprises and a few worries. The song began playing once again in her head.

Amazing Grace, how sweet the sound that saved a wretch like me…

Whoo hoo, she said to herself, I've got a new job. A warm house and hot water. And my baby's asleep in his bed. She lay back to fully cover herself with the calming, soapy bath water. In short order, she felt drowsy and put her nearly empty glass on the rim of the tub, giving in to her fatigue.

It had been a very full day.

She didn't hear the knock on her front door, but Gene did. He got out of bed and opened the door to Sister and her baby, saying come on in, he'd get his mom. Still half-asleep, Gene knocked on the bathroom door. Pauline didn't hear the knock or the noise that ensued: baby crying, Gene shouting for help, he and Sister pulling her out of the tub, and dragging her to bed.

So much for her celebration: she'd passed out in the bathtub.

They all laughed about it the next day.

"Sorry you had to see my privates," Pauline laughed, calling out to Sister who was folding the blanket she'd used on the couch. Sister smiled and watched Gene playing with the baby.

Pauline launched into her third cup of black coffee, thinking about the day ahead.

CHAPTER THIRTEEN

Salvation

Not many from the little Freewill Baptist Church in Panama City were there for Billie's baptism in late August—just a couple of sisters and Roosevelt, her brother. After all, Billie had barely attended the church; just gone to occasional music conventions or tent revivals on a hot summer night, when there was nothing else to do. She had retired from the bar business and moved to Florida at 75, wanting to get away from the hard, cold winters in West Virginia, not realizing just how hot and humid Florida could be. The heat made it difficult for her to breathe. She spent most of her time sitting in her rocker, in front of the television and the oscillating fan, a man-sized handkerchief tucked between her large breasts.

Most of her siblings had moved to Panama City when Billie did. She was still the matriarch of the extended family, and they knew she'd watch out for them. Her sister Helen lived on the same street as Billie, four houses down, and being a few years younger and easier to push around, Helen drove Billie wherever she wanted to go and brought over dinner each evening. On this one muggy August evening, with nothing on television but Lawrence Welk and no air conditioning, Billie talked Helen into going to the singing convention under the tent two blocks away. Billie thought at least there would be fans around the inside of the tent.

Having had a Wurlitzer with neon lights in the dance hall of her beer business, Billie had listened to popular and bluegrass music most of her life and enjoyed old-timey music and hymns. She told Helen that different choirs from Clearwater and Jacksonville were singing at the convention. Helen agreed and she and Billie walked down to where the music had already started. Billie found a couple of empty seats on the aisle near the back and settled in, removing her damp handkerchief to wipe away sweat in the folds of her pale face and neck. The electric fans weren't making much of a breeze and Billie wondered if they should have stayed home. Helen commented that most people had fans with the funeral home logo on them. "I guess they ran out," she whispered to Billie. "I don't see any extras." Helen pulled at her skirt and spread her legs wide, hoping for a puff of air.

After twenty minutes or so, right after the preacher, a bail bondsman in town, started praying, the heat got to Billie. With eyes closed, she began to feel faint and veered side to side while standing with her head bowed. Helen didn't notice, but a church sister in the chair behind her noticed and touched Billie's shoulder, asking if she was feeling the spirit. Billie mumbled something that the church member took to be "yes," and she let out a loud shout, "Sister's got the spirit!"

Before you knew it, a dozen or so members swarmed around Billie, fanning her and praying loudly, touching her wet back, her sweaty arms and head, shouting "Thank ye, Jesus. Thank ye!"

The preacher rushed down the aisle and told Billie he'd pray with her. He eased her onto her black metal chair, knelt down in the aisle, holding her hands and began to pray out loud.

Helen wedged herself out of the row of chairs as Billie sat down. "This is too much," she thought. "I need a cigarette."

"What the hell is happening in there?" Helen said out loud, as she got a light from a heavily tattooed young man sitting on the bumper of an old Chevy outside the tent. "Same old thing," he replied. "Jesus saves!" Helen took a long draw off her Pall Mall and gave the man her best smile. Inside the crowd was shouting to the heavens, "Thank ye, Jesus."

It became a frenzy: old women kneeling at the altar speaking in tongues, their skirts flying up and over their behinds. Old men crying, leaning on their walkers and canes, blowing their noses into rags, wiping tears on shirt sleeves. Children running wild and screaming down the aisle, free of parental control for the moment. The choir hummed in the background, *Softly and Tenderly, Jesus is Calling.* The spirit ruled the night. Only Billie wasn't having it!

One sister offered Billie her handkerchief, and Billie sank down onto the altar step, her face buried in the somewhat dryer cotton cloth. She shook her head, not quite believing what was happening. She tried but couldn't locate Helen in the crowd. Damn that woman. Just when I need her, she whispered to herself.

Billie's pink house dress was steeped with wetness and her gray hair curled and tangled over her head. Her body was like a furnace, with all her body folds embracing the condensation. She kicked off her house shoes, raised and fanned her skirt out to cool off down there. She wasn't thinking clearly but hoped she'd worn her bloomers.

Soon another choir took the stage and began to sing in a rousing Motown way, a favorite altar call, *would you be free from the burden of sin? There's power in the blood.* The crowd parted a bit as people began to clap and sing along, moving aside to get some air for themselves. Billie asked for water, and someone handed her a warm Grape Nehi.

The preacher asked Billie if she had anything to say to the congregation—witness her salvation, as it were. This was a frequent opportunity to tell church members how sinful her life had been, the awful things she'd done to others and now, Jesus had shown her a better way, saved her soul.

"Nope," Billie said, as she grabbed her shoes and lunged for the side door, hoping to find Helen. "I just need to get out of here." Helen threw down her cigarette and ran to catch up with Billie walking barefoot on the road home. "How'd you get out," she asked. "Shut up," Billie told her, walking faster, "some friend you are!"

Two days later the preacher visited Billie at home to ask if she'd like to be baptized in the Withlacoochee River the next week, along with two others who had found the spirit that same evening.

Not certain if she'd been saved or not, Billie had been considering if this was it. Is this what being saved is all about, she wondered. No big revelation, no vision of Jesus, no sudden feeling of hope. She felt the same as earlier in the week. Maybe it'll come later, she thought. That feeling of grace. Maybe one has to grow in the spirit, she considered. Or maybe it's just a yes or no. Simple as that.

These were big thoughts for Billie, having never considered religion part of her nefarious life. Perhaps being saved was simply a decision, she considered, not a transformation. A decision to try and follow Jesus' way, as told in the old family Bible where everyone's birth date had been recorded.

Billie looked at the Bible, now on the coffee table, then at the gray-faced bondsman preacher. Being dunked in a cool river sounded so good to her on this blazing August afternoon. Nodding to the preacher, Billie said, "Might as well go all the way."

The water was cool as Billie stepped into the river. The bondsman preacher and another deacon from the church assisted her into the waist deep water, both holding her arms.

The preacher raised his hand to the heavens: "Jesus, we commend this sister to your grace. Bless and keep her safe, in your name."

They lowered Billie under the water, then brought her up.

"Whew, that felt good," she said as her face came out of the water. "Wish I could stay here all day."

"Hallelujah," the preacher shouted. "Another soul for Jesus."